Soul Alliance

Reading Order

Big River pack:
Gray's Wolf
Micah's Match
Emory's Mate
Reed's Girl
Tristan's Voice

Blackwater Clan:
Colton's Kitty
Noah's Fire
Carter's Devotion
Luke's Redemption

Ravenwood Pride:
Braxton's Warrior
Aron's Element
Daxon's Heart
Mason's Princess

Morse Pack:
Koda's Challenge
Auddi's Destiny
Zeke's Revelation

Shifter Council Executioners:
Shift in Priority
Shift in Focus

Other Titles by Lynn Howard:
Soul Surrendered
Laken (Immortally Yours)
Zac (Immortally Yours)
Her Heart to Mend (A Contemporary Romance)

Soul Alliance

Lynn Howard
@2022
Published by Twisted Heart Press, LLC

Valdis crept through the woods, the string pulled back on her handmade bow as she stared down the length of the arrow. It had been weeks since any of her Clan had had meat. They had solely been surviving on the meager vegetables they'd been able to harvest over the fall and stored deep inside the cave in which they were currently residing.

A single rabbit wouldn't fill the bellies of the more than a dozen people in her Clan, but it was better than nothing. They needed the protein the hare would provide.

A crack of a twig to her left caused the animal to twitch. And then it took off in the opposite direction in a full sprint. There was no way Valdis could hit him while running.

When several more cracks of twigs and crackles of leaves met her ears, she realized she, too, should turn tail and run.

Someone was coming.

As quietly as she could, she ducked through the thick brush and ran for the cave. She needed to warn the humans she had lived with over the years. It wasn't the first group of humans she had joined since her family had been killed when she was a child. And probably wouldn't be the last. They didn't live as long as her kind. But they were still her people, and she cared about them.

Members of the Clan were spread about the area where they had attempted to create a home, where they thought they would finally be safe enough to build a life and raise the few children who had been born.

A few started hard when she burst through the brush.

"We've got company. Get inside," she whispered harshly, still running as she made her way inside to beg those within to hide.

They had learned to keep fires burning only within the caves to avoid being detected by either the glow at night, the scent of the wood burning, or the smoke that would rise in the sky.

"Someone's coming. Hurry. Get further inside, find somewhere to hide," she ordered.

Diving for her sword, she pushed away those who begged her to stay within and away from danger.

The humans were far more vulnerable than Valdis. It would take a lot more to kill her than it would them. And she was as adept with a sword as any of the grown men in the Clan.

"Stay inside," one of the older men said, shoving her back.

"Bullshit," she said, pushing past him and toward the mouth of the cave.

She was small, but had had to learn to fight at an early age when she was left to fend for herself. She'd learned to fight first with her bare hands, then with weapons.

No one argued any further. They merely moved further from the cave opening and spread into a semi-circle, hoping to hold off anyone looking for women to steal for breeding purposes.

When the world had been splintered into regions after the human war, most of those who had survived the nuclear bombs had moved south. It was paradise, so warm and beautiful, and the grounds were easy to grow food.

But as in every group of humanoids, there were those who would exploit others for their own greedy reasons.

One of the consequences of the nuclear fallout was the inability for a majority of non-humans to procreate with their own. They now needed human women to carry their offspring to continue growing their numbers.

Since the time the groups began to split off, commodities like food and water had replaced any other currency. The second most important commodity were women, specifically humans.

As the Elves took over and developed monarchies to draw up and enforce laws, two factions arose – the *Ihllr* and *Vhtir*. The Ihllr were as close to evil as one could get. Perhaps not truly evil, but their only goal in life was to take what they wanted, consequences be damned.

The *Vhtir* now ruled the northern region of Ahdlai, where humans fled in droves as the Ihllr continued to hunt them.

But they weren't the only risks living in the forests. There were so many creatures now that would feed on the humans or others caught wandering at night. No non-human was forced into hiding any longer, and rejoiced by terrorizing any weaker or more vulnerable than themselves.

The sounds of approach grew louder. The enemy wasn't bothering to hide their presence. They hoped to create enough fear to make the humans panic. Panic caused people to run, and predators always preferred to chase their prey.

But Valdis wouldn't run. She would never run from these assholes nor would she ever show them an ounce of fear. If she would be struck down, she would go down fighting.

The first of the Ihllr Elves appeared through the thick brush, a sneer on his face. As a child, Valdis had always believed the bad people would resemble monsters. That they would be easy to discern from good people.

But the men who flooded through the trees didn't look monsters. They could even be considered handsome – if it weren't for the fact they were there to take slaves and slaughter anyone who got in their way.

Holding the sword tightly in both fists, she glared at the men striding toward them as if there weren't seven men and Valdis prepared to fight them off.

But Valdis knew it was pointless. There were at least ten of them, and there could have been more in the woods that had yet to appear. The human men wouldn't be able to fight the Elves off. And Valdis could only take on one or two at a time.

"That's cute," one of the *Ihllr* said. "You could save yourself some grief and put down your weapons. Or, we could kill every single one of you and still take your women."

A rage burned hot in Valdis's veins. She sure as hell wouldn't allow them to take her anywhere. She would rather slit her wrists right then and there than allow them to use her for some sick plan to add to their harem.

As much as she wanted to rush forward and thrust her blade as deeply into the asshole's stomach as possible, she didn't want to risk starting the battle if there was a way she or the others could talk their way out of it.

"There are far more than you see," Valdis said, hoping a bluff would be enough to sway the Ihllr from their attack.

The Elf who'd spoken lifted his head and his nostrils flared as he scented the air.

"There are only a few more, and they are all cowering behind you in that cold, damp cave. Wouldn't your women prefer to live in luxury?"

"Fuck you," one of her Clan's men said.

"Luxury? Is that some form of joke? What world do you live in where you think being taken against your will and raped repeatedly until you deliver a child is considered luxury?" Valdis said.

She didn't bother hiding her hate for these men. She didn't bother keeping the anger from her voice as she stared down each Ihllr one by one.

But she wasn't an intimidating person. She was barely a few inches above five feet while the smallest of these men stood at least six feet tall and was packed with so much muscle they could easily crush Valdis's skull with little effort.

It didn't matter. It didn't matter that she was no match for these men. She would do her best to protect the humans who had taken her in and allowed her to become a part of their Clan. She would fight until her last breath to give the women inside the cave time to run or hide.

Movement in her periphery made Valdis tense a moment too late.

A band clamped down around her arms, immobilizing her upper half. That band was of the warm, muscled type.

She thrashed and kicked at the same time the humans from her Clan sprung into action and began to do their best to hold off the Ihllr Elves. Valdis watched in horror as one by one, they fell under sword or dagger, their blood soaking into the early spring forest floor.

Ducking her chin, she shot her head backward, hoping to make contact with the nose of the man holding her prisoner. But with her height, she only succeeded in smacking the back of her skull against his chin and mouth.

It was enough for him to loosen the hold on her; enough to slip away and swing her sword in a wide arc, dragging the razor-sharp edge across his middle.

There was no time to ensure he was down. She had to face off with those at her back and do her best to keep the remaining men from her Clan alive.

She was able to inflict several wounds and effectively took down two more Ihllr before she was knocked to the ground from behind.

Stars erupted in her vision.

No. She couldn't allow her body to give up, not yet. She would not be taken by these assholes. They had no idea she couldn't give them heirs. But would that matter or would they simply find another use for her and her body?

Pushing to her feet, she searched for her sword but her eyes refused to focus. She would have to fight with her fists.

When the next *Ihllr* came near her, she thrust her hand out, palm up, and made contact with his nose. He slapped his hands over his face with a grunt of pain and stumbled back a few steps.

But there were still far more of them than she could take on and the men from her Clan were now lying dead on the ground, their eyes staring lifelessly at the macabre scene around them.

As she squared up to the asshole in front of her, she was yanked off her feet by a hand wrapped in her hair. Several pops preceded the pain as small chunks of hair were ripped from her head by the roots.

When the first foot made contact with her stomach, knocking the wind from her lungs and preventing her from drawing in another breath, she realized she would fulfill the promise she had made to herself: She would die before she let anyone use her as their own personal sex slave.

Chapter Two

Jhelan used the shirt of an *Ihllr* to clean the blood from his sword and shoved his weapon into its leather sheath. The enemy had been wandering far over the border of Ahdlai too much lately. They were hunting for females and slaves and didn't bother with formalities like laws.

Because word travelled fast throughout the different Clans and groups of humans, they were learning to stay as far from Mhahzin as possible. Which meant the *Ihllr* had to get creative – or destructive, depending on how one saw it – to find those with whom they could breed.

A sound met his ear. A whimper. A feminine cry of pain.

"Do you hear that?" Prince Ahrkyn asked.

The sound was coming from Jhelan's left, no more than a few feet from where he stood.

Pulling his sword free once more, he crept toward the sound, the prince and a few guard members flanking him on either side, ready for battle.

They hadn't seen any females fighting with the *Ihllr*, but it wasn't uncommon for the males to bring their mates along during raids or hunts.

Checking the position of the other men, he nodded his head once then shoved a large clump of brush aside.

There were no *Ihllr* members hiding, waiting for the *Vhtir* guard to leave. Instead, there was a small female curled in a ball, her face and body battered and bruised and covered in blood.

The eye not swollen shut rolled toward him and her body tensed. She pushed up until she was on her knees, grabbed a large fallen branch, and brandished it as a sword, ready to defend herself.

Was this who the *Ihllr* had been hunting? Had Jhelan and the other *Vhtir* guards arrived in time before they were able to abscond with the woman? By the looks of her, she had put up one hell of a fight, but there was no way she could have won in the end. She was half the size of any of the *Ihllr* hunters.

As Jhelan dropped his sword to his side and reached for her, she swung the branch, guttural growls escaping her bloody, split lips.

"Who is she?" Prince Ahrkyn asked.

"How would I know?" Jhelan muttered.

"Feisty thing," Ihsander, one of Jhelan's closest friends, said with a chuckle.

The four guards, consisting of Jhelan, the prince of the *Vhtir* Elves of Ahdlai, and two of Jhelan's closest friends, sheathed their swords then stared down at the woman, unsure of what to do next. They couldn't very well leave her in the woods in this state. She might not make it through the night with the temperatures dropping as the day stretched on. It would be weeks before the evenings would rise above freezing when spring finally arrived.

The scent from her blood indicated she was more than merely human, but he couldn't discern whether the halfling had Fae blood or something else.

Slow, steady steps from approaching horses announced the arrival of the rest of the guard who had joined in the perimeter check and resulting battle.

"Did you miss one?" a male asked from atop his horse.

"She's injured. She appears to be a victim," Ahdeben said, still staring down at the woman who shot daggers from her eyes. Well, one eye since the other was barely visible through the swelling and bruising.

The damage done to her body would have been by severe blows. Whether she fought back or not, there was no reason to inflict so much damage to such a small woman.

"We can't leave her here," Prince Ahrkyn declared.

"I agree," Jhelan said.

"Take her to the Palace, have the healer check her over, then take her to your home."

Jhelan whipped around to gawk at the prince. "What? Why my house? Why can't she stay with someone else? Or in the Palace?"

"Because she is Unclaimed and Untouched. You know the rules. And you're the one who discovered her. That makes her your responsibility."

"You were all here, too."

But the prince merely stared at Jhelan with his icy blue eyes until Jhelan sighed and moved forward to lift the woman from the ground.

While the connection and friendships between Ahrkyn, Jhelan, Ihsander, and Ahdeben went back as far as their wet nurse, the prince's words were final. Jhelan could balk and protest all he wanted, but he would lose the argument in the end.

The woman swung the branch, but lost her balance and pitched forward. She was weakened and thin, as though she hadn't had a decent meal in weeks. Perhaps longer.

Jhelan lunged for her out of reflex and caught her before she could land face first on the forest floor.

She continued to fight as he lifted her against his chest, pitching her over his shoulder so he could mount his own horse, but her struggles were no more effective than an infant's.

Once he was situated in the saddle, he lowered her so she was practically straddling his lap, her head limp against his chest.

Turning a frown on Ihsander, he sighed when his friend indicated she was no longer conscious.

At least she couldn't fight him if she was no longer awake. Hopefully, the healer could tend to her well enough to be able to send her on her way quickly. Surely, she would want to reunite with her Clan.

"Stupid people," Jhelan muttered.

"What? What are you complaining about now?" Prince Ahrkyn asked.

"These people are given the opportunity to live within any of the towns but prefer to struggle in the forests and live in caves. And it's obvious they don't bathe. She stinks," Jhelan said, lifting his head in hopes of putting more distance between his nose and the woman's body.

It wasn't that he didn't pity the woman's situation, but she and others like her had chosen to live in the wilderness, at risk of discovery by so many creatures, so many enemies to those who chose to live like animals.

"Could we drop her in the tub before taking her to the healer? I'm not sure how much longer I can stand the stench."

"How is that any closer? Show some compassion and focus on your duties," Prince Ahrkyn said.

"Since when did my duties include allowing an Unclaimed woman to reside within my home?"

Ahrkyn pulled the reins until his horse slowed to a stop, then turned a look full of authority on his friend.

"You found the woman. She is your responsibility. That is the law."

"Why can't we tell your parents someone else found her? Or we could leave her near the town so another will stumble upon her."

The prince made a sound in the back of his throat of pure disapproval but kicked his horse and continued on their path.

They had slaughtered the *Ihllr* they'd discovered, but that didn't mean there were no more lingering in the woods. They would still need to remain vigilant, but Jhelan was at a disadvantage. He would have to find a way to keep the woman safe before he could dismount and join any battle that might erupt.

Being as the prince demanded Jhelan take responsibility for the woman, perhaps Jhelan would keep his ass right there in the saddle and let the rest of the guard handle any problem that arose.

For a brief second, Jhelan wished for an attack, something to help prove his point that bringing this woman along was a hindrance.

Each of the guard members, as well as adult *Vhtir* Elves, were expected to Claim a human, but only if she was willing. They would fill their mate's belly with a child, sire an heir, then allow the woman to return to the life she left behind if she so chose. Or she could remain in a home provided by the Royal Family rather than scavenge for food and struggle to survive among all the creatures that inhabited the woods, both wild and paranormal.

Jhelan vaguely remembered the time before life was as it was now. He vaguely remembered when the humans ruled the planet, barely remembered the war they had waged among themselves. When their civilization had been nearly wiped out and the number of them was far below those of the paranormal world, those like Jhelan's parents and King Nhaeem had stepped in to take over and now ruled the entire world. They rebuilt a government in hopes of protecting those more vulnerable.

Each region was broken into monarchies with very clear lines of territory. Only an invitation directly by that region's king or queen permitted entry, and those invitations were rare.

But the *Ihllr* of Mhahzin had long since ignored any and all rules or laws set forth by the Fae, Elves, or Shifters. Their numbers had greatly increased due to their act of taking women from various regions and breeding with them.

Thus the need for constant patrols and battles.

Jhelan had long ago requested an attack on the *Ihllr*. But King Nhaeem and his Queen Ahlmeda preferred diplomacy over violence.

He feared that would one day bite them in the ass when the *Ihllr* far outnumbered the *Vhtir* and were able to overthrow their leaders.

Keeping his horse positioned in the middle and near the prince, flanked by his two other closest friends, Jhelan reached down to settle the woman again. Her head lolled with each step of the horse and continued to roll off his shoulder.

She smelled of sweat, forest, dirt, and blood.

But there was an undercurrent of her natural scent there, something not unappealing. Something that stirred a sensation he couldn't identify deep in his gut.

He pushed it away, and tamped down the desire that hardened his body when her own pressed against his crotch in the most tantalizing way.

Had this been any other situation and any other woman, he would prefer to be naked. But this woman was now his responsibility, meaning he was tasked with tending to her and keeping her safe until she was healthy enough to be on her own.

As if he didn't have enough with his Royal guard duties.

By the time they reached the edge of town outside the Palace walls, Jhelan nearly sagged with relief. He needed this woman away from him. And that urgency was no longer simply because of her stench.

She was doing something to him, something odd to his insides. And he wasn't sure he wanted to entertain exactly what those odd sensations were.

"They have returned," someone announced loudly.

The bell was rung, alerting the town and Palace of their presence.

"They've brought a prisoner," a woman said with nothing short of confusion.

Prisoners were rare, and would never be cradled against a guard member's chest

"She is not a prisoner," Prince Ahrkyn announced, shushing all rumors that had already began to filter through the growing crowd.

Mates of fellow guard members smiled as their men flooded by. Some held rounded bellies. Others were merely happy to see that the person they'd been tied to for the time being had returned to them alive.

Jhelan had no one waiting for him. He hadn't since his parents' deaths.

All he had was this filthy, bloody, broken woman leaning against his body.

Pain. Blinding pain. It pushed out any and all thoughts of anything but the agony burning through every nerve ending in her body.

No matter how hard she tried, she couldn't find an end to the searing of every cell in her body, nor could she force a sound from her lips as a scream bubbled up in her chest.

Why wouldn't it end? Why couldn't she find any form of light at the end of this hellacious tunnel?

Why couldn't she just die?

A sound broke through the sawing of air into her lungs, through the pounding of her heart loud in her ears. A sound Valdis was unsure whether she should celebrate or dread.

A male voice spoke somewhere nearby. She had heard that voice before but couldn't recall the memory, couldn't quite place it. The voice sent both adrenaline and peace throughout her body, quelling some of the pain.

But not quite enough.

"We found her during our run," the man said.

"Was she in this condition?"

"Yeah. She was still conscious, though. She tried to fight us with a stick."

There was obvious humor in the man's voice.

Why was that funny to him? She'd had no other weapon and refused to allow anyone to drag her away. They had already killed or kidnapped every member of her Clan.

She was alone in the world. Again. She had long ago lost her family, but members of that Clan had taken her in when she was barely in her teens. They had treated her as part of their family, as though she'd belonged there.

And now she had no one.

Something cool and wet touched her forehead. Valdis bit back a moan as the touch caused an injury to sting and ache. As long as these people believed she was unconscious, she might have been able to glean enough information to discover where she was and how she could escape.

"She was still fighting when you found her?" the woman asked.

"Trying to. She couldn't have swatted a mosquito. She was too weak."

"I don't understand how she was still awake. Her injuries are extensive. Many cuts will require stitching. She will have scarring. And her right foot is broken. I'll have to immobilize it to prevent any further damage."

There went any chance of escape. If she had a broken foot, there was no way she could outrun whoever was holding her.

She'd thought she had successfully fought off the *Ihllr* Elves who had tracked her, beat her, and laughed in her face when she continued to climb to her feet, refusing to give up so easily. She had been fueled by rage and sorrow at watching her people slain at their hands, and hoped to take at least one of the enemy with her into the afterlife before she fell.

The cool cloth continued to rub along each gash on her face, her scalp, arms, and legs. She had no idea how much damage she had inflicted upon her opponents, but hoped they felt at least half as badly as she did.

Doubtful. They had towered over her and were heavily muscled while she was thin from the scarce food supply she and her Clan were able to find.

The woman continued to bathe the drying blood from Valdis's skin. The man continued to grumble and complain about having better things to do.

"So, leave her with me. I'll send for you when she is ready to be moved."

"Prince Ahrkyn has put her in my care. I am not to let her out of my sight unless on duty."

There was a beat of silence as the woman's gentle hands moved to Valdis's foot.

Pain caused white flashes to erupt behind her eyes as the healer moved her foot, then secured something hard on both sides.

When a belt or some fastener was tightened, Valdis could no longer hold back. She moaned long and loud, barely swallowing back a scream.

A man's face hovered in Valdis's vision.

"What is your name?"

"What?"

"Your name."

Valdis could barely think past the pain as she tried to remember her name or think of anything past the nausea roiling in her stomach.

"She's almost done. Focus on me. Tell me your name. Tell me about your Clan."

"Valdis," she said through clenched teeth.

"Where is your Clan? Tell me about them."

While Valdis appreciated what the guard member was trying to do, she could no longer hold back when her bones rubbed together and a splint was secured tightly to her leg. A scream tore from her lips and her back bowed as she tried to find a way to escape the pain.

"Can you give her something to dampen the discomfort?"

Discomfort. Either this man had never broken a bone or was far tougher than Valdis would ever be, because what she felt was far from discomfort.

Valdis saw the woman move out of sight then reappear with a cup in her hand. The man took it and slid a hand under Valdis's head to raise her enough to sip the liquid.

It was bitter and warm as it washed over her tongue and down her throat. There could have been poison in that cup and Valdis still would have drank from it, as long as she was able to escape the throbbing and fire licking at her nerve endings.

As the man pulled the cup from her mouth and slid his hand out from under her head, his eyes stayed glued to hers. His were a striking blue, much like the sky on a spring morning, so blue they were nearly ethereal. Fae? Elf? Definitely not human. There would be no humans on the Royal guard. And the leather battle vest with the emblem of the region was evidence of his position.

His dark brows and raven hair made his eyes appear as beacons, drawing her in, begging her to drown in them as her lids grew heavy and her body relaxed.

She didn't want to sleep. She wanted to discover where she was and avenge the murder of her Clan. She wanted to hunt down those who had put her in this position and inflict the same damage to their bodies they'd done to hers.

Or maybe they were already dead. The guard must have been hunting any who had crossed the border into Ahdlai. Perhaps that was why the *Ihllr* had ceased tormenting her and left her lying in a heap in the brush. Which meant she was right in the center of this region's capital.

This man had told the healer Valdis was now his responsibility, that the prince had deemed it so.

She didn't want to be his responsibility. She wanted to climb from this bed, disappear into the woods, and let fate take over. She should have died alongside her people. The guilt of surviving while they had been cut down was nearly as painful as her broken bones.

"It's working," the healer said.

She moved closer and bent over Valdis, a needle poised in her hand.

"Will she feel it?" the man asked.

"She shouldn't feel much as the elixir courses through her system."

Fingers were on her forehead, pinching the broken skin together. Valdis barely registered the sting of the needle piercing her skin before those cerulean eyes were focused on her again.

"I am Jhelan," he said. "You are in the region of Ahdlai. Can you tell me where your people are? Where your Clan is located?"

"They're dead," she said, her numb lips struggling to form the words.

"Your Clan was slain?"

"Yes."

"The women?"

"Dead or taken," she said as tears burned the backs of her eyes.

Her body might have been numb, but her emotions were far from it. She suddenly wished for the physical pain to return so she could focus on it rather than the grief shattering her heart and constricting her throat.

A tear rolled from the corner of her eye and soaked into her hair. She couldn't hold it back nor could she stop those that followed as she remained unmoving, staring into a set of eyes that both hypnotized and frightened her.

She didn't know this man. Didn't know whether he was the enemy. Didn't know whether he had ulterior motives.

But for now, he was her anchor, the only thing she could cling to while at the mercy of the healer using needle and thread to put Valdis back in one piece.

Even with the cuts stitched, it would be weeks before she would be strong enough to walk out of this place on her own. She couldn't very well hobble out with only one good leg.

She had to wonder why the prince cared whether she was healthy or not, why he demanded Jhelan be responsible for her care. Once citizens of Ahdlai declared themselves outsiders and chose to live away from the sprawling town, they were forgotten by the Royal Family, discarded, left to their own devices.

Which, of course, was the point of living outside of the towns.

Most of the people living in the forests and caves were human. Valdis happened to be of Fae blood, but still chose to live among those who considered themselves free. She would rather hunt for food than beg for scraps from those who deemed themselves superior.

Now, Valdis was literally at the mercy of the very same people she had rejected and avoided her whole life.

Jhelan backed away as the healer moved further down Valdis's body, checking each wound.

"The others can be bandaged. But ensure she keeps them clean."

"Can she bathe?"

Valdis's brows puckered as she followed Jhelan around the room with her eyes.

"Dry the stiches immediately, and rebandage the other wounds as soon as they're dry."

"Thank you."

Jhelan said nothing as he reached down and slid one arm under Valdis's back and the other under her knees. As much as she wanted to protest and demand he set her on her feet, her body was still numb and not cooperating with her brain from the elixir.

"Bring her to me in a few days so I can ensure she's healing well. Do not let her put weight on that foot. None. Otherwise, I may have to perform surgery and prefer to avoid that."

Yeah. Valdis preferred to avoid that, as well.

She could put no weight on her foot. Meaning there would be no walking on her own, at least not without some form of aid or assistance.

Jhelan was ordered by the prince of Ahdlai to watch over. How long would she be dependent on the man who looked as though he would rather carry a wild animal than Valdis?

She lost track of the path he had taken her through the Palace but, eventually, they stepped into the cool evening air. Her exposed skin chilled instantly and she wished she hadn't lost her cloak while fighting the *Ihllr*. Or had she donned it at all? The memory of mere hours earlier felt as though she was trying to see through murky water.

Jhelan glanced down at her, then hugged her tighter to his body while keeping his head high. It appeared he no longer saw any need to distract her or make eye contact with her as he carried her through the large garden encircling the Palace grounds and through the front gate.

Valdis ignored the curious glances thrown her way as he continued to walk through paths and brick laid streets until he stopped in front of a house close to the edge of town.

He shifted her so he could free one hand and turn the knob, pushing the door open with a foot.

She was instantly surrounded by his scent. She was also instantly warmer as the breeze was cut off by the closing door.

Jhelan carried her straight to a bathroom nearly the size of the last cave her Clan had inhabited. She was a child when the humans had destroyed the planet and their own way of life. But she remembered the luxuries of that time. Like the large shower in one corner of the room and the deep garden tub beside it.

If she couldn't put any weight on her foot, a shower was out of the question. At this point, she didn't care as long as she could sink into warm water and wash away the blood encrusting her hair.

Carefully, he sat her on the vanity top and moved around the room, pulling bottles and towels from cabinets and closets. Then turned to leave.

"I…"

He stopped in his tracks and looked at her over his shoulder when she spoke.

Valdis glanced down at her foot then back up at Jhelan.

He cursed under his breath, then crossed the room to turn the taps and fill the tub. As carefully as he had set her down, he lifted her and set her on the edge of the tub, then stepped back.

His hand was rough, his movements agitated as he pushed his fingers through his hair and ran his eyes up and down her body.

"Hope you're not modest."

Then he moved forward and gently began to peel the clothing from her body, his eyes on her face the entire time.

The moment her breasts were bared, she crossed her arms, covering them the best she could.

He helped her to one foot, closed his eyes, and lowered her breeches to the ground, urging her to sit so he could pull them over her feet, careful not to jostle her injured foot.

Eyes still closed, he lifted her and bent, settling her in the tub and below the water and growing bubbles before lifting his lids.

"I'll send a servant to aid you further."

She gaped at him for a second.

"You could have sent a woman to undress me?" She didn't hide the anger in her voice.

"I hadn't thought of it at first. And it's been a while since I've seen a woman's body."

Her nostrils flared as she glared at his retreating back. What an arrogant ass.

He hadn't seen her body unless he had peeked as her tunic had covered her face when he'd pulled it over her head.

Jhelan obviously resented her for being in his home, as if she had a choice. He resented the fact he was now responsible for her care, resented the fact he'd been ordered by the prince to play nursemaid.

If he was going to be a jerk to her, she would make sure she gave him as much grief as he gave her. She hadn't been beaten nearly to death for being submissive.

If he thought her presence in his home made him miserable before, it was going to get a whole lot worse if he didn't start treating her a little nicer.

Chapter Three

Jhelan practically stomped the entire way to the servant's quarters. He could have asked a female neighbor for help, but the servants were specifically hired to aid the Royal Family and guard. It was literally their job to help with things like bathing a strange woman inside Jhelan's home.

"You look happy," Ihsander said as he passed.

"Fuck off," Jhelan replied.

Ihsander chuckled as he continued across the Palace grounds and toward his home. By now, the guard and the prince would have reported their findings to the King and Queen. They would have told the Royal couple all about the woman in Jhelan's house and cemented his duties of being her caretaker.

There was a reason Jhelan had chosen to avoid Claiming a female and siring an heir – he wished to care for no one but himself. He had no desire to dote on a woman while she carried his child and no desire to raise an infant, though he'd have help from the residents within the town in the center of Ahdlai.

Regardless of his resistance, he had still been sidled with a woman. Oh, and she wasn't even *his* woman. Simply someone who would need him to wait on her literally hand and foot until she was healed enough to walk.

Sometimes, Jhelan couldn't help but wonder if Mother Universe had a sick sense of humor. Or perhaps hated him for some unknown reason. Because he sure as hell always seemed to get the short end of the stick.

Elabeth, one of the longest serving women in the Palace, was leaving the quarters as Jhelan descended the stairs.

"I need your help," he growled out, then turned and expected her to follow.

He had never been one for small talk, but he normally wasn't so rude to the Palace staff. He also never had a shitstorm tossed into his lap, either.

"Yes, sir," she said, her steps hurried as she jogged to keep up with Jhelan's long legs.

By the time they arrived back at Jhelan's home, Valdis's head was leaned against the side of the tub and her eyes were closed.

Shit. Had she died in his tub when he was supposed to be watching over her?

Reaching forward, he touched two fingertips to her throat and jumped back when she jerked awake and swung a bruised and damaged arm at him.

"Good. You're not dead. This is Elabeth. She'll help you bathe."

With that, he turned on his heel, pulled the bathroom door closed hard enough to rattle windows, and stomped outside to sit on the front stoop.

How the hell was this his life? How had the prince thought he was the best choice to care for an injured woman? Jhelan hadn't technically been the one to find her. They had all been crowded around when they'd heard her whimpers and moans of pain.

Jhelan must have done something to piss off the prince. And instead of approaching his friend with the problem, he turned Jhelan into a nursemaid.

People milled about, closing up their homes, locking their animals in pens for the night, lighting lanterns and closing gates. There was a reason the guard members were positioned at the edge of town. It was the first and best line of defense against anyone who dared to wander too close to the Palace.

Ahdeben wandered over, a half-eaten apple in one hand. "I hear she's awake."

"How did you hear that?" he asked sarcastically.

The people nearby did everything they could to avoid looking in that direction. No doubt word of not only Valdis's presence but her condition had made it to every set of ears within Ahdlai.

Ahdeben chuckled. He leaned against the side of Jhelan's house and joined in watching the people prepare their homes for evening.

"Why do you think Ahrkyn tasked you with her care?" Ahdeben asked. And if Jhelan wasn't mistaken, a twinge of jealousy colored his words.

"I must have pissed him off. Otherwise, I have no idea. He knows I'm the worst person in this kind of situation. I'll kill anyone you want, but have no clue how to care for an incapacitated person. And especially not a woman."

"Have you discovered what kind of halfling she is?"

"No."

Had she not been bleeding so profusely when they'd found her, they might have missed the subtle difference. But the air was thick with the coppery scent. That same scent clung to him since the woman was occupying his only bathroom.

Turning to look up at Ahdeben, he opened his mouth to ask to use his shower when the front door opened behind him.

Elabeth's head peeked through the crack.

"She requests you, sir." She stepped back inside, leaving the door open.

"Of course she does," Jhelan muttered under his breath as he pushed to his feet.

He was weary. His muscles and joints ached from battle. But he couldn't rest. Not until the woman was sound asleep.

He cursed inwardly when he realized he would have to give up his bed for the duration of her stay. His couch wasn't large enough for her to stretch comfortably while her foot healed. And there was no way he could stretch comfortably, either.

Elabeth stood at the open doorway leading into the bathroom as Jhelan stepped inside. Valdis was no longer in the tub, but sat on the side with one towel wrapped around her middle and another draped around her shoulders. Her hair was dark from the moisture, but looked as though it would be dark blonde or light brown when dried.

She no longer held the stench of the forest and blood. In fact, that undercurrent of something he had detected while she'd ridden cradled against his chest was stronger. And damned near intoxicating.

"What is it?" he asked, wincing at his tone. He hadn't meant for the words to come out so harsh, but the situation had put him in a foul mood.

"I don't want to be here," she said, jutting her chin and squaring her shoulders the best she could.

"There is nothing I can do about that."

"You don't want me here. I don't want to be here. Find somewhere else for me to stay while I heal and then I'll be on my way."

Jhelan opened his mouth to say how great of an idea that was, but something stopped him. As much as he'd detested the thought of another person invading his space, as much as he had hated the thought of caring for this woman until the prince deemed her healthy enough to leave…he didn't want her to go.

He couldn't explain it. Not to her, not to himself, not to anyone.

She was now his duty. He didn't have to like it, but he would complete the assignment, ensure she was well fed and healed. Then, he would await instructions from the prince or his parents as to where to take the woman.

"No," he said.

"What?"

"I said no. You'll stay here. Elabeth will find you some clean clothing. After you're dressed, she'll make you a meal and then you can sleep."

"If she's the one doing all that, why can't I stay with her?" Valdis asked.

There was fire in her one visible eye and her jaw was set like she was ready for a fight.

"Because she shares her quarters with the rest of the staff. You are not staff. You are a guest and under my protection."

"So then *you* should be the one who has to fetch me some clothes and *you* should be the one who has to cook for me."

Jhelan narrowed his eyes. She thought he was low enough in rank to run around finding women's clothing? Or to stand over a stove while she watched and waited for her meal? He was the head of Ahdlai's Royal Guard. Not a damn servant.

She was goading him. Provoking him. Trying to get him to want her to leave.

Okay. Fine. He'd been through enough years of psychological training while in guard training to beat her at her own game.

"Where will I find clothing to fit the skinny woman?" he said, adding the jab in and smirking when she rolled her eyes.

It wasn't a secret that the Elves in Ahdlai preferred a woman with curves. There was something about the dips and valleys of a woman's rounded belly, wide hips, plump ass, and large breasts that set their blood on fire.

Or perhaps it was being brought up within the Royal palace that made him believe the thicker women were of higher class and unlike those who dwelled within the caves.

Elabeth's eyes widened and her brows shot high up her forehead.
"Sir?"

"Where?" he said.

She blinked a few times and jerked her head for him to follow. Before closing the bathroom door, he turned to smirk at Valdis.

"I'll be back to get you dressed then cook you some dinner."
"Wait—"

He closed the door before she could protest.

Yep. He would be the one to dress her. He would be the one to remove the towels from her body and pull a clean tunic over her head. He would figure out some kind of meal that held enough nutrition to help her body heal, then he would tuck her into bed.

Maybe after a few times of him getting an eyeful of her naked body, she would drop the attitude and allow Elabeth to do what she was hired for.

Valdis would have thrown something at the door if she could have reached anything other than the towels wrapped around her body.

She was now sitting practically naked, waiting for Jhelan to return with some clean clothes. And since she'd opened her big mouth, he would be the one to tug them over her head.

She had hoped to point out that he had no business caring for a woman since he had zero idea of what he was doing. He held no marks on his arm, so he wasn't Fate Claimed. He could still have a mate in the town somewhere carrying his child, but he sure as hell didn't act like he had ever taken care of anyone other than himself.

The bath had eased her tense muscles, but the soapy cloth Elabeth had used to clean her had abraded her many open gashes and scratches, causing them to sting anew. The elixir had officially worn off.

The worst pain was when the servant had washed the blood, leaves, and other things from Valdis's hair. Elabeth had been gentle, but it had still throbbed and stung.

Her foot had hung over the side of the tub awkwardly the whole time. That foot wouldn't be washed until the healer removed the binding.

When was the last time she had enjoyed the feeling of being truly clean? Easy answer – it was before her family had been slaughtered and she had escaped into the woods. Since that day, she had only bathed in the river, but never with anything scented as she had today.

Time ticked by as she continued to sit on the edge of the tub, clinging to the towel Elabeth had wrapped around her middle, tucking the ends between her breasts. The woman had then draped another around her shoulders for an extra layer of warmth.

But enough time had passed that neither towel warmed her any longer. Her wet hair gave her a chill and she began to shiver.

The door wasn't that far. Surely, she could hop on her good foot to at least get close to the hearth and warm herself by the small fire there.

Or she could slip and fall flat on her face. Then Jhelan would find her and probably laugh at her idiocy. He seemed like that kind of person, the kind who laughed when someone tripped rather than help them to their feet.

More time passed and her feet and hands began to feel like ice. He was taking his time on purpose, causing her to sit there and wait for him. He knew she was unable to fend for herself and wanted to prove she needed him.

Bullshit. She didn't need anyone. She had been on her own for a few years after her family had been killed and her first Clan had found her.

Pushing to her feet, she reached out and grabbed the edge of the vanity for balance. She made sure to keep her broken foot raised to resist the temptation of setting it on the ground.

One hop. Two. Only a few more hops and she would be to the door.

On the third hop, the door swung open. Valdis squeaked in surprise and jumped, causing her to begin to sway backward. She was going to either land hard on her butt or hit her head.

But warm, strong arms wrapped around her upper half and pulled her upright.

"What the hell are you doing?" Jhelan barked out.

He scooped her into his arms and carried her to a bedroom, dropping her hard enough onto the mattress that she bounced a little, jarring her battered body and reminding her of wounds that had finally stopped aching.

She didn't cry out, didn't moan, didn't make a noise. She didn't want him to know he had caused her any form of discomfort, didn't want to give him that satisfaction.

Jhelan left the room and returned with an armful of colorful fabric, dropping it all on a heap beside Valdis.

"Drop the towel," he barked.

She simply tightened her grip on the towel wrapped around her.

"You plan on wearing that beneath the tunic? Because I have no problem with that."

"My foot is broken. Not my arms."

"Your arms are riddled with cuts, scratches, and bruises. I highly doubt you could raise either of them high enough to pull the tunic over your head."

To prove him wrong, she raised both in demonstration.

And he took the opportunity to yank both towels from her and toss them in the corner.

As Valdis struggled to cover as much of her bare body as she could, Jhelan struggled to shove her arms into the tunic sleeves without further injuring her.

"Just...stop," he said, his voice softer than it had been.

It was also a touch deeper than before.

With a sigh, Valdis dropped both arms to her side and let him dress her as though she were a child, coming just short of a full pout.

He tugged the tunic until it hit the mattress below her. She would have to stand to pull it the rest of the way down.

He then stood with a pair of wool pants and stared at her legs.

"I don't have a clue how to get these up your legs without hurting you further."

He said it as though he were thinking out loud rather than speaking directly to her. The fact he was concerned about causing her more pain earned him a half of an inch of her gratitude. But he was so deep on her shit list she wasn't sure he would ever be able to dig himself out.

"We'll have to forgo the pants for now."

And just as he had in the bathroom, he scooped her into his arms before she had the chance to open her mouth and carried her into his dining area, depositing her on the chair. He was more careful this time and didn't simply drop her onto the hard wooden chair.

"I've never cooked for anyone before," he said, his back to her as he pulled various ingredients from different locations in his house. "Don't blame me if you get sick. I don't keep much food in the house."

Whether it was his words or her current situation, a giggle bubbled up in her chest and escaped through her lips.

Jhelan turned and frowned at her over his shoulder. "What's so funny?"

Valdis threw her arms out to her sides. "This. All of this. I have no one. I'm officially dependent on someone who hates me. And once my stupid foot is healed, I'll go back to the woods to live like a nomad and scavenge for food and run from the monsters and..." Tears thickened her throat and cut off anything else she might have said.

Jhelan watched her for a few more seconds then sighed. He set the vegetable he'd held in his hand on the counter and crossed the room to sit in the chair beside her.

"They're all dead?"

"If they're not dead, the *Ihllr* have them. That's as good as dead."

"Did your brothers fight? Was that why they were killed?"

"I have no brothers. My parents were killed when I was a child. My first Clan took me in as a young girl. They were all killed. This Clan accepted me, took me in, treated me as one of their own. And, yes, the men were killed trying to protect the women and girls of my Clan." A sob shook her body. "I have no one," she whispered.

Something akin to pity or perhaps compassion flashed through his brilliant blue eyes. And then was gone just as fast.

Jhelan pushed to his feet and returned to the counter to cut vegetables in silence. Valdis allowed the tears to flow freely as she watched him move around his kitchen, preparing a meal for a stranger he had found in the woods.

"My father was killed when I was young. He was a member of the guard. He was killed while on duty," he said softly, his back to her.

He was trying to comfort her in the only way he knew how – empathy.

"I was raised here in Ahdlai."

"You've never lived elsewhere?"

"I've travelled. But there is no better place than here. It's why I have dedicated my life to protecting its people and the Royal Family."

For a moment, Valdis began to see Jhelan as a man rather than a jerk. She could almost see his heart on his sleeve. It was faint but there.

Until he finished cooking and dropped a bowl of some form of vegetable soup in front of her. Liquid sloshed over the side and onto the table, but he ignored it and fetched her a spoon.

He made his own bowl and took the chair across the table instead of beside her. He also ignored her the entire meal, keeping his attention solely on the food in front of him until he'd finished the solids and poured the last of it down his throat as though the bowl was a cup.

Manners weren't something any of those who resided in the forests cared about so she wasn't exactly appalled by his behavior.

As he set his bowl down, he cocked a brow at her, almost a challenge for her to mention the way he ate.

Okay. They were back to hating each other. So be it.

Valdis finished her vegetables, then did as Jhelan had and tilted the bowl back, drinking the last of the liquid. She then set the bowl on the table and leaned back in her seat, raising her brow at him as he had her.

A grunt was his only response.

"Are you ready to sleep?"

She was tired. Beyond tired. It was more than the physical exertion wearing her down but the emotional, as well.

The prince had said she had to remain in Ahdlai until she was healed. But she knew it would take far longer for the cracks in her heart to mend than it would her bones.

"I can crawl," she said.

His brows dropped in confusion. "What?"

"I can crawl to bed. You don't need to carry me everywhere. I know you think I stink. I know you think I'm stupid."

His brows lowered further.

"I heard you. When we were on the horse. I was fading in and out, but I heard you. So don't worry. I'll take care of myself from here out. I'll keep my stinky body as far from you as possible and refrain from saying anything stupid."

She wasn't making sense. She knew she wasn't making sense. She was speaking out of anger and grief but couldn't seem to make herself stop.

Jhelan didn't interrupt her. He leaned against the back of his chair and folded his thick arms across his barrel chest. Each of the guard members she'd seen since waking within the territory looked as though they were bred from giants.

"You're going to crawl everywhere. Like a child," he said rather than asked.

Out of everything she had said, that was the one thing he clung to. He didn't deny saying she smelled badly, didn't deny referring to herself and those who chose to live outside of the monarchy as stupid.

With a huff, she turned in her chair, set one foot on the ground, then lowered to her knees. And then began to move forward only on her knees, one slow shuffle at a time as she made sure to keep her foot raised from the ground. It was slow going and the skin over her kneecaps began to burn and her joints ached, but she refused to stop now. She would not ask that asshole for help.

By the time she made it to the bedroom, every muscle in her body screamed in protest. She had to use the side of the bed to climb to her one foot and drop onto the bed, her breathing labored as though she'd been running.

A deep chuckle sounded from the doorway.

Valdis turned a glare his way, but the smile didn't falter from his face.

"I'm impressed," he said. Then blew out the single candle sitting on a dresser and closed the door behind him.

His heavy footsteps echoed on the hardwood as he moved away from the room.

Steadying herself, she scooted and maneuvered her body until her head was on the pillow, then pulled the thick bedding up her body until it was tucked under her chin.

She hadn't slept in a real bed in decades. She'd almost forgotten how soft and warm they were, had forgotten how comfortable they were.

But she wouldn't get used to it. Couldn't get accustomed to the luxuries she would experience while within the territory of the King and Queen.

Valdis stared at the dark ceiling until her lids grew heavy and her thoughts slowed. She knew the *Vhtir* was of no threat to her, but she couldn't shake the feeling that she wasn't fully out of danger. Perhaps it was her Fae blood sending her a warning. Perhaps Mother Universe was trying to warn her of impending danger.

Perhaps the Universe was warning her that Jhelan could be dangerous.

She just didn't know whether he was a danger to her body or her heart.

Chapter Four

Jhelan laid on the couch, his legs hanging over the side starting at his calves. That tiny waif of a woman didn't need his bed. She would barely take up a corner when fully stretched out.

He could always wait for her to fall asleep, creep in there, and retake his bed. If he woke early enough, she might never know he was there.

But if she had lived in the forest as long as she'd said, she would wake at any and every sound. She would be vigilant, even while resting.

His luck, she would flail at his appearance and tear open her stitches. Then he would have to bring her back to the healer. He needed sleep. He needed rest. He needed to let his body heal itself after their long hours fighting the *Ihllr*. Spending hours with her with the healer wouldn't allow enough time for him to let his body recover after the battle.

He still hadn't showered. He had wet a cloth and wiped away the visible speckles of blood that had colored his face and exposed parts of his arms. But he knew he smelled as badly as she had when he'd found her.

She didn't smell bad now. She smelled of his soap and a scent that was uniquely hers, that same scent that had hardened his body and caused his heart to race as they'd traversed the thick woods on their way home.

Why had the prince chosen Jhelan to care for this woman? Ihsander would have been a much better choice. He had the kind of heart meant for this type of shit. Not Jhelan. Never Jhelan.

Rolling onto his side, he bent his knees and tried to fit his entire body on the couch. Most of the furniture his kind and others had used after the war had been what they'd found in the abandoned or destroyed homes no longer used by humans. Since then, they had begun to build their own to their tastes, had begun to manufacture and sell clothing and other goods. Unlike the earlier human society, most of the wealth now revolved around trade. The more you produced, the more wealth you accrued.

Jhelan didn't need wealth. Everything he required to exist was provided by the Royal Family in exchange for his service. Being a member of the guard was what he'd been bred for, trained for, and lived for.

And siring an heir was nowhere on that list.

Fabric rustled and the mattress squeaked in the bedroom. Lifting onto his elbows, he looked over the back of the couch and listened for any signs of distress. His luck, she would need to use the restroom and he would have to carry her.

Although, she was doing her damnedest to prove she neither needed nor wanted his help.

Fine by him. He was beyond ready to have his life back to the way it was before he had heard her pitiful sounds of distress.

When silence once again engulfed the house, Jhelan relaxed against the cushions and closed his eyes, surprised when sleep didn't immediately pull him under. Normally, after a battle like the one they had fought today, his body would shut down the moment his head hit the pillow.

But this wasn't a normal day. He wasn't in his bed and had no pillow. He didn't even have a blanket to cover his body, not that he needed one.

He had added logs to the fire to increase the temperature in the house after he'd found Valdis shivering as she had tried to hobble her way from the bathroom. The house was warm enough she could now sleep naked comfortably if she wanted.

His body hardened instantly at that thought.

It was nothing more than his need to sate the needs he'd ignored for so long. It had been weeks since he'd lain with a woman. Weeks since he'd felt the tight heat of a woman wrapped around his cock.

And thinking about the lack of intimacy was doing nothing to quell the desire building deep in his belly.

Valdis should have been the last person on his mind when it came to sex. She was badly injured, her face battered and nearly indistinguishable. And it was obvious she hated him.

Tomorrow, he would approach the prince and request she be moved to another home. It didn't matter how much the thought of her in another male's care sent sorrow and a touch of rage through his system. It didn't matter that he respected her strength and sense of survival. She was a hindrance to his life and his job. A burden he didn't want.

Of course, the more he thought about her staying in Ihsander's or Ahdeben's bed, the more that odd rage built until he sat straight up on the couch and fought the urge to pace.

What the hell was going on in his head? This was not him. He was not the mating kind. He didn't seek a woman to Claim. He had no desire to sire an heir.

And he sure as hell had no desire to Bond with one. The Fated Bond was rare, yet happened. And that would completely derail every aspect of Jhelan's life.

The only light in the room was from the fire burning in the hearth, the flames casting a warm orange glow throughout the room.

The bedroom door was closed. Would the heat make it to Valdis, or would she wake cold?

"Fuck," he growled under his breath as he pushed to his feet.

As quietly as possible, he padded barefoot to the door and opened it enough to reach a hand inside. The air was cooler there than in the living area.

She would freeze if he left the door shut through the night, even with his thick bedding wrapped around her small body. She had very little meat on her bones, giving her no natural insulation from the elements. And since he still wasn't sure what kind of blood flowed through her veins, he was unsure whether she was capable of regulating her temperature as some beings could.

He would assume from her behavior after bathing that was not one of her gifts.

Jhelan reached forward and pushed the door open further, just enough for the warmth of the flames to make its way inside and drive away any cool air.

That small gesture gave him comfort. Whether he wanted this task or not, he had always put his all into anything assigned to him. And that would include watching over this slightly annoying, impressively strong woman.

He took a moment to look her over. She was tightly bundled under his bedding, her head resting on his pillow, her body relaxed with sleep as her breathing came in slow and steady pulls. She had fought against the *Ihllr* and had survived. Not many could do such a thing. But this tiny woman who couldn't stand more than five-feet-three or four inches tall had. She'd endured many injuries, but had accomplished what she'd sought – she had avoided being taken.

Yet she'd lost her people. Had lost her Clan. She said she had no one. She would have nowhere to which she could return when her body was healed and the prince allowed her to leave.

Perhaps the people of Ahdlai would welcome her, show her the life she could have within the town, he mused as he returned to the sofa. Then she would have a new Clan. She would have a home and could make friends.

And Jhelan wouldn't have to let her go.

That last thought came as sleep drug him under. And he no longer had the strength to fight against his desires nor the Universe guiding him toward his destiny.

Jhelan had never believed in prophetic dreams. And he truly hoped his resistance in belief would mean he could manifest a different outcome.

He had dreamed of Valdis. Only she didn't appear as the woman who slept in his bed. She was a beautiful woman in his dreams. Her hair was the color of honey, her eyes the color of clover. Scars appeared as pale pink marks in places on her face.

But none of that was what he cursed Mother Universe for. No. It was the branding that had run from her left shoulder to her fingertips. The same brand that would appear only as silvery lines to others while appearing as dark lines to him.

They were the brands of the Fated Bond. The marks so few mated couples carried. A male could Claim as many women as he wished throughout his lifetime and never see those marks.

But the King and Queen both carried them. One member of the Guard carried those silvery lines on his arm, as did his mate.

They were the marks only given to those the Mother deemed anointed. Blessed. Sanctified. And the Bond was unbreakable.

Surely his dreams were merely a manifestation of his fears.

The sun peered through his windows and sounds of his neighbors filtered through the walls. People would be leaving their homes and fulfilling their duties, whether they worked in the garden, farmed, or worked for the Royal Family. All had roles to keep their community running as smoothly as it did.

No sounds came from the bedroom. Peeking through the gap in the door, he ensured she still slept, then quickly headed for the bathroom. No way could he go through another day with the stench clinging to him.

Water pounded tile as steam rose. Pushing his battle breeches down his legs, he next tugged the shirt he wore under his leather vest over his head. Every move pulled his sore muscles taut.

Focusing on the sounds in his home once more to ensure Valdis wasn't attempting to move around on her own, he stepped under the hot spray with a sigh.

The water instantly began to loosen the knots in his shoulders and back.

Jhelan put his hands against the tile and lowered his head, letting the stream form a wet curtain of his hair. He kept it tied back while on duty, but it felt so much better when he let it hang loosely down his back.

As much as he wanted to spend the next thirty minutes lounging in the shower, he needed to wash quickly and check on Valdis. She would need breakfast and a change of clothing.

She very well could have dressed herself last night. She had proven it when she'd successfully raised her arms over her head. Although he knew that movement must have caused her immense pain.

But he'd relished in provoking her temper. Her cheeks flushed when she was angry. And the eye that wasn't swollen nearly shut flared with a flash of emerald iridescence. It was as though she was a warrior trapped inside that petite body.

The water swirling down the drain went from red, to pink, then finally clear as he cleansed the day before from his hair and body. Turning the handles, he ended the spray and grabbed a towel hanging on the door.

Had the towels that had been draped around Valdis's body been left in the bedroom he might have used those. He would have held them to his face and inhaled her scent deep into his lungs.

Fuck. He had to fight whatever it was that was growing inside of him. He had goals for his life as guard to the Royal Family. And those goals didn't involve a mate.

Had the healer been gifted with regeneration, she might have been able to use her magic to heal Valdis faster, thus getting her out of his home and, hopefully, his head faster.

Though he knew forgetting a woman who awakened emotions he thought dead or dormant would be nearly impossible.

Once he was dry, he groaned. He hadn't bothered grabbing any clean clothes before stepping into the bathroom. He would have to leave the room with the towel wrapped around his waist and pray the woman still slept.

No such luck.

As he pushed the door open, she was sitting up on the bed, her eyes instantly going wide at the sight of Jhelan standing in the doorway half naked.

"What are you doing?" she asked, that fire reigniting in her eyes.

Even in her condition, she was prepared to fight off a male who might force himself on her.

"Getting clothes. Trust me, you're not my type," he grumbled, grabbing clean breeches and a shirt from one of the dresser drawers.

Why had he said that? Why did he constantly find the urge to goad her? Why did he constantly look for ways to provoke her?

Because when she was angry, she was...sexy.

How would she look when she was healed? Would it be as it was in his dream? Her hair, cleaned last night, was the honey color he'd seen in his sleep. But he would have to wait until her face was fully healed to determine how closely she resembled the woman he saw while he slept.

He turned to leave the room, intent on dressing out of her sight, but he couldn't take his eyes from the bruising that was changing to an angry purple. She'd needed stitches. She had a broken foot. Those fuckers had beat her so badly she would have died had the *Vhtir* not discovered her.

The *Ihllr* held no honor. The thought of injuring a woman, even the enemy, made Jhelan sick. He'd fought many an *Ihllr* female, but had always merely incapacitated them, never beat them senseless or killed them.

For a moment, the urge to find those who'd hurt Valdis and kill them all over again nearly took his breath. Had he known the atrocities they'd committed, he would have ensured they died slowly and painfully.

"What?" she asked as he continued to stare.

With a shake of his head, Jhelan gave her his back. "I'll make you breakfast after I dress. But wait for me this time," he said with a chuckle. "You're going to make your injuries worse if you continue to crawl around."

She couldn't see the grin that had stretched on his face as he walked away. The sight of a grown woman crawling on her knees to prove her independence was a sight he might never forget. He had stayed close behind, staying silent so she wouldn't hear him, in case she needed help. Just because he didn't want her in his home didn't mean he wanted her to incur any further injuries.

He would probably be blamed if she did.

As he pulled his clothes into place, he once again went over and over in his head why Ahrkyn would choose Jhelan for this job. It was customary for those in Ahdlai to care for those they discovered were in need. It was part of their code. The person would become responsible for the victim.

But there had been four men standing there when Jhelan had pulled back the brush and found her. He should not have had to shoulder the full burden.

It took him a few minutes to get his temper over the situation – and his dream – under control before leaving the room. And he couldn't hide the smile when he found Valdis on one foot, her hand gripping the side of the dresser, as she attempted to dress herself.

She was thin. Too thin. Far thinner than any woman he had slept with. But he could tell she would be beyond alluring after a few weeks of healthy meals.

And suddenly found himself wanting nothing more than for his dream to be prophesy.

Valdis was determined to change clothing before Jhelan reentered the room. Seeing him in nothing but the towel made her body warm and tight in places she refused to acknowledge.

He was such an asshole. And he was adamant there was nowhere else she could stay while she healed.

It was probably a lie. He was probably one of those sadistic types who enjoyed seeing a woman in pain. As long as she was dependent on him, he could verbally accost her at every turn.

The second she heard the bathroom door closed, she pushed off the bed as quickly as her body allowed and struggled to pull the tunic over her head without causing further damage to her body or tearing the stitches. She really didn't want to have to go through that again, with or without the elixir.

She held on to the side of the dresser, standing in nothing but the skin she was born in, and was reaching for one of the tunics Jhelan had deposited on the dresser before leaving her alone in the room when he stepped back into the bedroom.

His eyes went wide a moment, then a grin stretched on his face, like a predator ready to pounce on its prey.

"You couldn't wait, could you?"

"I can dress myself," she said, no longer bothering to cover her nudity.

He had already seen everything. What was the point of feigning modesty now?

One hand on the dresser, she lifted the tunic and tried to maneuver it so she could get an arm through a sleeve.

Stupid broken foot. Stupid *Ihllr* for hurting her. Stupid *Ihllr* for taking everything from her.

The pain in her body and heart warred for attention as she fought the tears that welled in her eyes. Jhelan had shown his contempt for her clear as day; she refused to show him any more weakness.

"Here," he said in a gruff tone.

He practically yanked the tunic from her hand and held it up so she could slide first one arm then the other through the sleeves before he tugged the rest over her head and settled it over her body.

"You still can't wear pants. You'll have to wear a cloak while we're out."

She frowned at him. "Where are we going?"

"I want the healer to check you over again. You seem to be healing quickly, but you're also stubborn and could have jostled the binding on your foot while showing the world how big and strong you are last night."

Anger burned hot in her veins as she glared at him.

When he bent to lift her into his arms, she swatted him away and hopped a couple steps back.

"Let's get all this out now, shall we?" she said.

"Get what out?"

"You don't like me. I don't like you. Neither of us are happy about this situation. How about we agree to keep our distance as much as possible? I won't talk to you. You don't talk to me unless necessary. Then, when your almighty prince declares I'm able to leave, you'll never have to see me again. Deal?"

Something flashed through his eyes as it had last night. Anger? Disappointment?

She was too tired and in too much pain to decipher or care.

"Deal," he said after a few moments of simply watching her. "Do you need any more help?"

"With what?" she asked.

He pointed to her head. "Your hair. The women around here wear braids. They adorn their hair with various items."

"I don't think I could get a brush through it let alone braid it. Not without busting the stitches."

Jhelan tilted his head and studied her head then disappeared through the bedroom door. When he came back, he carried a brush in one hand.

"I said I can't—"

"I'll help you. It's my duty."

"Your prince told you to watch over me while I heal. Not brush my hair."

"It's my duty," he repeated.

Fine. The jerk didn't want to budge. She would stand there and let him do his best to work through the knots in her hair. She was tempted to cry out if she felt even the slightest bit of discomfort for no other reason than to bother him.

He jerked his chin toward the bed.

"What?" she said, her face the picture of innocence.

"Sit. I don't want to have to hold you up while tending to you."

Valdis snorted as she tried to refrain from laughing. Tending to her. As though he were rendering first aid rather than pulling a brush through tangles and knots.

She hadn't seen herself in a mirror but imagined her hair resembled a bird's nest. She didn't want to think about how her face looked. It would do nothing but bring back the memories of yesterday's attack and her Clan's slaughter. She needed to refrain from showing any emotion. At least while Jhelan was around.

Fighting the urge to continue standing simply to watch his impatience grow, she hopped to the bed and lowered onto the side. The mattress dipped behind her as Jhelan climbed onto the bed and carefully touched her scalp.

His fingers were gentle, tender, as they ran along the line of thread where the healer had sewn her flesh back together.

Jhelan laid his palm directly over the wounds and slowly worked the brush from the end of her hair to the top. It took longer than it normally would, but she normally wouldn't have a stranger brushing her hair for her while sitting on his bed.

When he shifted his weight and slid a leg on either side of her, she became overly aware of how close their bodies were. She could feel the heat rolling from him, could feel his hardness through his pants pressed against her back.

His body had reacted to hers. But he was a man and she was an Unclaimed woman. There was no attraction between them, only simple primal chemistry.

By the time the brush began to move toward her scalp, his movements had become even slower and his touch softer.

And she found her body beginning to react to his nearness. He needed to finish and move away from her. They needed space between them before he got it in his head she was his to Claim.

"I can't get any closer," he said.

Her heart began to thump wildly in her chest. There were many ways he could get closer, ways she refused to contemplate.

"If I do, I'll risk popping a stitch."

Valdis blinked. Then blinked again. He couldn't get the *brush* any closer to her *scalp*.

What the hell was wrong with her? She'd found the simple gesture of his caring for her untamed hair sexual? And, as much as she had protested inside her head, had not voiced her discomfort.

Because there was none. Not the kind that should matter most at the moment. Not the kind that the nearness of a man who held her freedom and life in his hands should matter.

"It's fine," she said, wincing at the breathiness of her words. "Thank you."

There. That was better. She had put enough venom in her words to remind him they were forced into a situation neither of them wanted.

Valdis's body jostled as he scooted away from her and climbed from the bed. When he bent to lift her in his arms, he hesitated with his face inches from hers and raised his dark brows as though waiting for permission.

With a roll of her eyes, she nodded.

Jhelan carried her through the house and into the kitchen. And the entire time, she struggled to ignore the scent rolling from his body. He'd used the same soap as she had the night before. But it was more than that. His natural scent seemed to soak into her every pore, to wrap itself around her like a warm blanket, to embed itself into her very being.

She tensed.

"Am I touching a wound?" he asked with a frown.

Unable to find her voice, she shook her head. She would never say aloud the things she had just thought. Not only did she refuse to entertain them, but he would laugh in her face, perhaps remind her of his contempt for her.

Setting her gently on the chair, he set about the kitchen, pulling eggs and vegetables from the pantry. He never turned to look at her nor did he speak to her while he cooked.

When he set the plate in front of her, he nodded once, then opened the front door and stepped outside.

And then she was left alone with her thoughts.

She didn't like the quiet. Not anymore. Not since she had found too many things for her mind to grab onto and torture her with. She would rather be beaten over and over again by the *Ihllr* than allow a single memory or thought to bash her brains the way they did now.

As she struggled to finish the meal Jhelan made, she couldn't stop the barrage of images that came every time she blinked. It was the same last night. The moment she closed her eyes to sleep, she saw her Clan being cut down, heard the screams of pain and fear as she had struggled to remain conscious. She could hear the women crying out when there was no longer a barrier between them and *Ihllr*. Could hear the children begging for help.

Now she also had this stranger, Jhelan, to possess her thoughts. His scent should not have affected her the way it had. She should not have been comfortable sitting nestled between his thighs nor enjoyed the feeling of his hand on her scalp or the heat from his body beating against her back.

She needed to leave. She must do whatever was needed to heal as quickly as possible so she could leave this place. She needed as much space between herself and Jhelan as she could get.

Yet she had nowhere to go, no one to whom she could return.

It was fine. She had been on her own before and she could do it again. She would simply survive and, if Mother Universe so decided, she would find another Clan to join.

Enough time had passed since Jhelan had walked through his front door that Valdis wondered if he would return.

She was done eating, though she had only been able to stomach less than half the food. She was grateful for a warm, nutritious meal, but the pain and sorrow she fought made her stomach roil with every bite.

She was tired of sitting at the table with nothing to do. If there was a book nearby, she could spend the time waiting engulfed in a story. Instead, she had two choices: She waited until Jhelan decided he would return and move her to either his small couch or his bed, or she did as she had done last night and crawl awkwardly on her knees.

But her knees were still raw and sore from her stubborn move.

As she was looking at the couch and trying to picture Jhelan's large frame crammed on it all night, the front door swung inward and Jhelan looked at her with something akin to surprise.

"For some reason, I thought you would have been trying to hobble your way across the house or out of town by now."

"Wishful thinking," she said, giving him a wry smile.

His lips twitched at the corners as he shook his head. "I've brought something so I won't have to carry you through town. I thought you would be pleased since you obviously enjoy my nearness as much as I do yours."

Yep. He hated her.

"Let me guess – you've brought a wheelbarrow to push me around."

This time, Jhelan didn't bother hiding his amusement and released a smile that nearly disarmed her. When he smiled like that, the kind that was genuine, his rugged features softened slightly. His striking blue eyes sparkled with mirth and the lines of disapproval between his brows smoothed to lend him an air of youth.

He didn't speak as he moved closer and lifted her from the chair, but his smile stayed in place.

"Better than a wheelbarrow," he said as he stepped through his door.

There, waiting in front of his house, was a pony as white as the snow. It was small enough for someone of her size and would prevent her from having to be carried everywhere. At least while they were outside.

"Can you ride?"

"Of course," she said, this time regretting her snide tone.

He had sought out a way to help her navigate through town without having to be in his arms...because he thought she didn't want to be in his arms. Or perhaps she was correct in the way he felt about her. Perhaps this pony was a way for them to keep their distance from each other while he performed the duty assigned by the prince.

The mare was beautiful, not a spot of color anywhere other than her brown eyes. Her tail flicked as she waited to go to work.

Jhelan lifted Valdis high enough to settle her atop the horse as though she weighed no more than a child. The guards were all huge, their muscles well-honed and trained for battle against any and all threats.

Still, she would have thought he would at least be breathless afterward.

Grabbing the lead, he guided the pony through the streets of town until they finally made it to the Palace walls. The gates opened as they neared, the scouts up top able to see who approached.

Silence stretched as the mare carried Valdis across the massive lawn and through the gardens. She wondered if she shouldn't find something to discuss, some small talk to dissolve the awkwardness. But if he had something to say to her, he would have said it by now. He had barely glanced in her direction and that was only to ensure she was still securely in the saddle.

If she were able to speak with a member of the Royal Family, she had every intention of requesting a different situation. She would even stay in the servants' quarters if need be. Anything to be away from someone who clearly detested her.

But did he? Did he truly hate her as much as she had conjured in her mind? Because he'd gone out of his way to find a more comfortable situation for her to traverse the town. He had given up his bed and crammed his large frame on his small couch. He had made her breakfast this morning, but she hadn't seen him take a bite of anything as of yet.

As of the moment she had awakened and learned of her whereabouts and conditions, he had put her needs above his own. Even if he'd been a bit of an asshole at times and spoken to her like she was a nuisance or a burden.

Which, of course, she was a burden. If he was taxed with watching over her, he wouldn't be able to leave with the guard on perimeter checks. He wouldn't be able to join in battle if any enemy parties were found nearby.

All he could do was stay by her side as she healed.

She supposed she could be a little nicer to him. A little more grateful. But she wasn't sure how much honey she could drip on her words if he continued with his gruff attitude.

From then on, she would match energies. If he was polite, she would be in turn.

And if he continued with his piercing words and spoke to her as though she were a child, she would make sure he regretted the moment he laid eyes on her.

Chapter Five

"Four of us found her at once. Why am I the one you've singled out?" Jhelan asked.

He had sought the prince, his supposed friend, while the healer checked on Valdis.

"Ahdeben is interested in Claiming a female. Ihsander will do his best to put a baby in the woman's belly the first chance he gets. You are the only one I trust to keep your distance from her and watch over her without causing her any more bull shit."

Jhelan opened his mouth then snapped it shut.

Two of his best friends were interested in siring heirs. They wanted to be tied to a female and continue their bloodlines. That was why the prince had chosen Jhelan, because he knew his friend had no desire for either of those things.

He had carnal needs like any other man. But he slaked those needs with females willing to spend a few hours with him with no expectation of anything further. They lived within the towns and used him for the same thing he used them – to scratch a proverbial itch.

"How is she?"

"She required several stitches along her scalp and forehead. One of her eyes is swollen nearly shut and bruising quickly. And her right foot is broken and has been bound by the healer. I've had to carry her everywhere…when she allows it."

The prince's brows lowered the same time a smile pulled the corners of his lips up.

"Allows it?"

"You saw her in the woods. She's even worse now. She's stubborn. And feisty as hell. If I didn't know better, I would think she was a Shape-Shifter."

"Have you discovered her lineage?" the prince asked.

"It hasn't come up."

"You could ask."

"And you could find someone better suited to care for an injured woman than myself," Jhelan retorted.

"I heard you dismissed Elabeth last night."

"I didn't. *She* did. She said if she was going to be forced to stay with me then I should be the one who had to take care of her. It was a bluff."

"And you called that bluff," Ahrkyn said with a chuckle.

"Sure as hell did. Elabeth helped her bathe, but I dressed her and tucked her into bed after feeding her dinner."

The memory of her crawling on her knees, each step slow and deliberate, forced an unbidden smile on his face.

She truly was unlike any woman he had met during his lifetime.

"Have you discovered why she was in the forest alone? Why the *Ihllr* had attacked her?"

"They slaughtered her Clan. Or at least most of them. You know they probably took the women for breeding. Those who didn't fight as hard as Valdis, anyway."

"That's her name? Valdis?"

Jhelan nodded.

"So, she has no one," Ahrkyn said, sadness entering his voice and eyes.

"According to her, her family was killed when she was barely a girl. She was alone until the Clan found her and took her in. So, yeah, she has no one."

"She has you. And the residents of Ahdlai."

"Until she's healed," Jhelan said, leveling a look on the prince. "You said she was here until she was healed and then she would no longer be my responsibility."

"She may choose to stay within the town."

"But she will no longer be my responsibility," he repeated. He needed the prince to repeat those exact words, to confirm that once the woman was healed Jhelan could return to his guard duties and hunt down and execute as many of the *Ihllr* bastards as he could before being cut down as his father had.

That was his destiny, to die protecting the Royal Family, to die protecting the residents of Ahdlai. He would settle for nothing less.

"She will no longer be your responsibility," the prince confirmed.

Jhelan released the breath he'd held while awaiting the prince's words.

"As long as my parents agree."

"Come on. You said I was responsible because I found her. Once she's healed enough to walk and defend herself, how does that fall on my shoulders any longer?"

"I'm not saying they'll want her to continue staying under your roof. But she's new to our community. If she chooses to stay after, they may ask you to be their eyes and ears. They may want you to keep an eye on her, make sure she isn't a spy of some sorts."

Okay. That he could get behind. That fell within the scope of his job. Though he knew she wasn't a spy. She didn't have that kind of heart. She was the kind of woman who fought to the death to protect those she loved.

She had fought until she was near death and still had lost those she'd cared about most.

He had focused so much on her external wounds that he hadn't thought for one second about how she might be faring after such a great loss. He was only close to the Prince Ahrkyn, Ahdeben, and Ihsander. Yet his heart ached each time they lost a member of the guard during battle.

These people, those who had been killed during the *Ihllr's* raid, were her friends, her adopted family. Surely, she must be sick with grief.

She had put on a mask of strength since waking in the healer's surgery. She had barely shed more than a few tears.

And he'd been antagonistic and nearly cruel to her. He had cared for her physically, made sure she was clean, had food in her belly, and a warm place to sleep. But he had shown her no kindness nor compassion.

He could never be like Ihsander who wore his heart on his sleeve. But he could at least treat the woman as he would one of his friends. He could show her at least a sliver of kindness, help her body heal while she struggled to heal the holes left in her heart by the loss of her people.

Heavy steps echoed against the hardwood floor, moving closer to the living area where Jhelan relaxed with Ahrkyn. Ahdeben rounded the corner, his brows furrowed.

"She doesn't like me," he grumbled.

"You met Valdis," Jhelan said with a smile.

"I merely greeted her and asked how she was faring. She told me to fuck off. I've never heard a woman use that word before."

"You've never met someone like Valdis before," he said, and realized a swell of pride had overcome him.

She had cursed Jhelan's friend, yet he was smiling and proud of her strength. Either she was angry with Jhelan or was in pain. And she had chosen to lash out with words rather than scream in agony or cry as others would.

Interesting.

Did that mean he would see any more tears glisten in her eyes? Or would she verbally accost him each time she was in some form of pain?

And could he take that abuse with a smile, or would he treat her as he did his friends when they lashed out at him when they had a bad day?

No way could he treat her as callously as he treated them. She didn't deserve what had happened to her, hadn't asked to lose everyone and become dependent on complete strangers. She had been trying to live her life, surviving each day in the woods, hunting for food, making fires to cook or keep warm.

How foreign his world must feel to her?

"Give her time. Treat her as though she were any other woman in town or the Palace. She'll see we're not the enemy," Ahrkyn said.

"What's the point? She'll leave when she's healed up. There was far too much hate in her eyes to want to stay here," Ahdeben said as he lowered onto the other end of the couch.

"It was pain, not hate," Ihsander said.

The three sitting on the couch turned to find Ihsander carrying Valdis into the room, a new contraption latched around her foot. This one was larger but looked as though it offered more protection from her stubborn need to move around on her own.

"I can speak for myself," Valdis said.

Her arms were crossed over her chest and her chin was jutted forward as she waited for Ihsander to set her somewhere.

"I hear you don't like Ahdeben much," Jhelan said.

"That guy?" she said, pointing at Ahdeben. "I don't know him. How can I say if I like him?"

Ahrkyn and Jhelan chuckled. Definitely unlike any female he'd ever met.

"Can you put me down now?"

Ihsander sighed and, if Jhelan wasn't mistaken, hugged Valdis a little tighter to his chest before choosing a winged back chair to deposit her.

A strange possessive feeling invaded Jhelan's thoughts. Why did Ihsander hug her tighter? Why did he feel the need to be closer to Valdis? That wasn't his right.

Ahrkyn had told Jhelan the male was looking to sire an heir. Any thoughts of coming near Valdis had better never enter the asshole's head or there would be consequences.

And Jhelan would be the one who doled out the punishment.

Valdis pushed the new wave of pain away and focused on the four men staring at her.

"What?" she said, raising her brows.

Just like with Jhelan, she would show them no weakness. Ihsander had been kind and gentle when he had offered to carry her from the surgery, but he was still one of the people keeping her here.

Not that she had a choice at the moment. If the prince were to exile her, or if they were to open the gates and welcome her to leave on her own, she wasn't sure she could do more than crawl a few feet before collapsing from exhaustion. And there was no way she could hunt for food in her condition, especially without her tools or weapons.

She had already determined she would use the time here to build her strength up and heal before leaving. There was no reason to make enemies of every single guard member and resident of Ahdlai in the meantime.

Problem was, she had never been an overly affectionate person to begin with. When one lives a portion of their lives alone, it becomes hard to grow attachments.

She had allowed herself to form attachments after losing her family, had allowed her heart to feel for the first Clan then the second who had taken her in. And then lost them as well.

It didn't bode well for her heart.

"Is there anything we can get you, Valdis?" the prince asked.

All eyes widened and turned to her. They looked as though they feared she would curse their leader.

She was in pain and angry, not stupid.

"I'm fine. Thank you," she said.

Both Jhelan and Ahdeben looked surprise as they shared looks of amazement with each other.

"Why are you nice to him and not me?" Ahdeben asked.

She rolled her eyes and tried to cross her legs at the knee. When she winced, Jhelan leaned forward, his hands outstretched.

What had he planned to do? Lift her and carry her around again? There was nothing he could do but give her body and heart time to heal, then he would be rid of her.

"Are you hungry? I can have one of my staff bring you something. Or we can go to the dining room if you would be more comfortable there."

"I fed her," Jhelan said.

Valdis snorted, then sucked her lips into her mouth to hide her smile when Jhelan gave her a confused and disgruntled look.

"Did I not?"

"It was food," she said.

The three men turned their heads to look at Jhelan.

"Why is Elabeth or someone else not preparing her food?" the prince asked.

"She said she didn't want their help."

That wasn't technically what she'd said. And she had believed by putting the sole responsibility of her care on his shoulders he would ask for her to be moved. It hadn't happened yet, but it had only been a day. Maybe after a few more days of him waiting on her hand and foot, he would throw up the white flag and ask for Valdis to be moved to a woman's home for the duration of her care.

Prince Ahrkyn narrowed his eyes on Valdis with a slight smile on his lips as though studying her or looking for an answer to a question he had yet to ask.

After a few moments of Valdis refusing to lower her gaze, he pushed to his feet.

"We'll go to the dining room. You'll be more comfortable there."

And then he sauntered off, obviously expecting one of his subordinates to ensure she joined him.

When Ihsander stood and moved toward her, Jhelan lunged to his feet and practically pushed Ihsander across the room.

"She is my responsibility," he said. Or rather growled. There was anger and something else in his eyes and his voice as he glared at his friend.

Ihsander grinned unrepentantly and threw up his hands in surrender. He and Ahdeben left the room, presumably to join the prince in the dining room.

Once all three men were gone, Jhelan turned and looked down at Valdis. What was he waiting for? Did he expect her to push to her feet so he wouldn't have to bend over to lift her?

Fine. She didn't want to be there, but she didn't want to be any further of a burden than she already was.

Scooting to the edge of the chair, she set her good foot on the ground and used the arms of the chair to push to standing.

And yet Jhelan continued to stare at her, an unreadable expression on his ridiculously handsome face. She hated to admit it, but he had a sort of rugged beauty to him that was only intensified by his feral blue eyes.

When he didn't reach for her, she huffed and turned to hop on one foot in the direction the others had gone.

"Wait," he said.

She stopped and turned to look up into his face.

"I'm sorry."

"For what?" she asked. Her condition wasn't his fault. He'd killed those who had brutalized her and slaughtered her people.

"I've been an ass. This…situation is not your fault. And I've treated you as though you intentionally altered my existence. I vow to treat you with more respect from this moment on."

Valdis blinked a few times, staring up into his face as she sought the meaning behind his words and watched for any signs of deception.

There were none. And his meaning was plain as day. He had acknowledged his treatment of her and was promising to do better.

Which meant she, too, must do better.

"I'll try to be less of a pain in the ass."

That was the best she could do for now. It was hard to think any further past the aches and pain that radiated through every cell of her body and the hollows of her heart.

A slow smile stretched across his face, once again lending him an air of youth and innocence.

"Deal?" he said, repeating what she had said earlier that day.

"Deal," she agreed, unable to stop her own smile.

With nothing more said, he moved forward and scooped her against his chest with one arm under her knees and the other behind her back. Unlike every other time, she wrapped one of her own arms around his neck rather than crossing them over her chest and remaining stiff and rigid as he carried her out of the room, down the hall, and into a massive room with a table that could easily fit twenty or more people.

Ihsander, Ahdeben, and the prince were already at the table, chatting and drinking from glassware Valdis remembered her family owning. Or something similar to it. She was not born into a wealthy family, but they had been comfortable before the world had been flipped on its head.

Servants – or staff, as the prince had called them – flitted in and out of the room, carrying various sizes of trays and bowls, placing them all on the table.

It was far more food than five people could eat.

And as noise filtered throughout the house, she discovered why.

Several men, all as large and intimidating as Jhelan, entered the room and took seats around the table. As they conversed among each other, it seemed they, one by one, noticed her presence and all conversation slowly ceased until everyone was staring at her.

It took every ounce of energy in Valdis's battered body to refrain from glaring or blurting a rude comment. They were merely curious of the newcomer's presence.

Two more sets of steps softly echoed through the house until two more joined the large party in what Valdis thought was more a dining hall than dining room.

Oh crap. The King and Queen would be dining with them. Why had no one warned her? It was hard enough for Valdis to maintain her composure around the prince. Now she would have to mind every word she spoke with the entire Royal Family at the table.

She would not have expected them to lower themselves to dining with their employees. She would have thought the guard would have their own area to eat, or maybe a different time.

The Queen was beautiful. Almost painfully so. She was a halfling, no doubt, as most non-humans were. The only species capable of breeding among themselves were the Shape-Shifters.

But the non-human side of her must have been Elven. Her skin was like porcelain, the tips of her ears pointed and barely visible through her hair. Her eyes were an aqua blue, her lips full and painted red. Even the way she moved appeared as though she floated rather than walked.

The dress she wore made Valdis's borrowed tunic resemble a rag in comparison.

"Is this the young lady you found during your battle?" the Queen asked, her eyes focused on Valdis.

"Yes, Your Highness," Jhelan answered.

"And she has been put in your care? Has he treated you well, young lady?"

"Valdis," she said, then looked at Jhelan. There was nothing short of pleading in his eyes. "Yes; he has treated me very well."

"Good. I like to hear that. You look like you could use a few hot meals. And your injuries look atrocious. Has the healer tended to you yet?"

"Yes, ma'am, uh…Your Highness." She was unused to addressing someone so formally. There were no higherups in her Clan, no leaders. Everyone was equal and worked equally as hard to keep their little group safe and healthy. Or as healthy as one can be while living off the meager amount of wildlife left after the human war.

A few chuckles were covered by coughs.

"Very good. You should be good as new in no time. We have one of the best healers in this half of the hemisphere."

Of course they did. Because they were the rulers of the region of Ahdlai, a territory that, indeed, took up half the hemisphere on this side of the world.

There were four regions that spanned the planet. The northern region of Ahdlai, the southern region of Mhahzin, then on the other side of the world there was Fhatim and Ahde. Valdis had never ventured across the ocean and had lived in Mhahzin before their King had been overthrown and the region had been taken over by a dictator who would rather execute his own people than raise them up and increase their prosperity.

Plates were set before each person circling the table, starting with the King and Queen. They and the prince were served first, then Valdis's plate was filled before the servants moved on to the rest of the guard.

She was mildly surprised she was treated as more important than those taxed with the job of protecting the Kingdom and its residents.

Valdis couldn't help the trepidation that worked its way through her system as she stared down at the plate. She recognized the food, had tasted much of it as a girl. But it had been a long time since she'd had such fresh vegetables. And the desserts perched on a side table continuously caught her eye. She had not had anything so sweet since before she was left to her own devices in the forest.

If given the choice, she would forgo what was on her plate and dive face first into the cakes, pies, and other treats waiting to be enjoyed.

"Tell me of your Clan," Queen Ahlmeda said as Valdis continued to look longingly at the desserts.

"There is nothing to tell," Valdis answered.

The Queen stopped with her fork halfway to her mouth. "Do you not wish to speak of them, or…"

"They're gone. Either dead or taken."

"You were the sole survivor?"

"Yes, Your Highness."

Queen Ahlmeda set her fork on her plate and waved her hand in the air. "You are a guest in my home. You and your people have never declared yourselves members of my region nor sworn loyalty. You may forgo any formalities while in my home."

That wouldn't happen. Especially with the looks of astonishment on every face at the table save the King's.

"Do you have family elsewhere?" King Nhaeem asked.

"I no longer have anyone on this planet." She swallowed hard and blinked back tears that threatened to well in her eyes. "My family was killed long ago. And now the Clan who took me in is gone. I'm alone."

"And you wish to leave when you are healed?" the King asked. "Where will you go?"

Appetite quickly waning, Valdis pushed her plate away before she had taken a single bite.

"I don't know. But I'm sure there are others out there who would be willing to take me in."

"The invitation to stay within the town of Ahdlai is open ended. Should you decide you wish to remain after you are fully healed, simply tell Jhelan or my son and we will provide a home and find a job suitable for your skills."

Before the attack, she had aided others in protecting the Clan. She was adept with a sword as well as bow and arrow.

But she was also half the size of every single man sitting at the table, their heads wagging back and forth as they listened intently to the conversation about Valdis's future.

"Thank you," Valdis said. She had made up her mind that she would walk out of town and directly into the forest the first chance she had.

However, after only one day of the luxuries she'd long forgotten, she was reconsidering that decision. She would be given her own home and a job to earn her way in this place. She would be protected from those who hunted for the most vulnerable.

She would also be forced to swear her allegiance to the King and Queen and follow their rules, something of which she wasn't sure she was capable. She had never been great with following orders.

That little tidbit was the only reason she was still alive. When Valdis had warned everyone of the Ihllr's presence, the men in the Clan had ordered the women to the back of the cave. But Valdis was determined to fight alongside them, determined to do her part in keeping her people safe since she was harder to kill than the humans.

And now she dined with the Royal Family in the Palace, surrounded by tall walls and strong, capable guards of varying species and gifts.

Valdis's own Fae blood was too diluted. She had no gifts of which she was aware, none that would aid her in a fight. The only thing that she was thankful for was her healing would be more advanced than that of a human. It would still take her longer than she would like, but she would be able to walk on her own again within a couple weeks.

And then she would need to decide whether her freedom was more important than her safety.

Chapter Six

It had been two weeks since the day the *Vhtir* guardsmen had found Valdis broken and battered in the woods. In that time, her bruises had begun to fade to nothing and her stitches had already been removed.

Jhelan saw her differently than he had before. Her golden hair framed a beautiful face, her mossy green eyes were bright and wary of everything around her, her nose short and pert, and her lips were full and the color of the softest pink rose.

She had also done as she'd promised and attempted to rein in her anger, although it still peeked through at times.

They had developed a routine in their weeks together. He would help her to bed, leave the door open for the heat of the fire to make its way to her room, then crash in an exhausted heap on the couch. He had not been allowed to join the guard on hunts and perimeter checks, but he'd been tired to the bone from carrying the petite woman anytime the pony could not be used.

She had developed a habit of sitting up in bed and hobbling to the dresser to pick something loaned to her while waiting for him to wake and carry her to the bathroom.

There had been no more crawling. And she no longer did her best to pull away from him when she was in his arms, but instead wrapped one arm around his neck and leaned against his chest.

It had become the favorite parts of his day and he began to think of more and more reasons he should carry her rather than lift her onto the back of the small, white mare.

"I want to walk today," she said as he settled her at the table.

He had learned to cook more than the bowl of vegetable slop that he'd fed her the first few days, yet she still requested to eat in the Palace at times. He suspected it had something to do with the sweets the staff served at each meal.

"Your foot is still bound. Until the healer –"

"So, let's go see her today. I'm going to grow weak if I can't use my body. Survival is impossible for the weak."

That simple sentence slashed through his heart. She was still considering returning to her life in the forest when this was over. As much as he had detested the thought of having her in his home that first day, he'd grown used to her presence.

No. He'd grown to appreciate and enjoy her presence. She was still feisty, still had a foul mouth at times, but was witty and intelligent.

More intelligent than he had believed the tree and cave dwellers would have been.

"You said you entered the woods when your family was killed. Do you remember the time before that? When you were with your own people?"

Valdis looked at the table and rubbed her finger along its surface. She was silent so long he wondered if she would answer.

"We lived much like this," she said, looking around his home. "But our house was bigger. There were eight of us, so we had to have more space."

"Your parents had six children? They remained together after you were each born?"

She snorted and shook her head. "Not everyone abandons their mate after childbirth."

As much as Jhelan wanted to argue, she spoke truth. Once the woman gave birth, she was no longer a part of the child's life, at least in the Elven culture. She may choose to remain in town, but she no longer resided with the man who mated with her nor did she have any say in the child's upbringing or assigned role for his or her future.

"You've never told me from what bloodline you derive."

She glanced up at him then back down to the spot where her finger smoothed. "Fae. I'm a Fairy halfling. Or a thirdling? Both my parents were Fae, but my mother was a halfling."

He nodded and returned to his chore of making her breakfast.

"What about you?"

"I was told I was Fae growing up, but when my ears changed…"

He pushed his long hair aside and showed her the point at the tops of his ears.

Her brows rose. "I don't think I've seen your ears since coming here. I've seen…other parts of you," she said as her cheeks reddened, "but never your ears. Do you hide them on purpose?"

Jhelan sighed as he chopped a chuck of meat. "It's an old habit. I grew up with the Fae. My family did their best to hide their Elven traits before finding King Nhaeem and the others. Before the human war, Elves were seen as tricksters, thieves, and liars. Kind of like the stupid stories the humans told in their fairy tales."

"I'm sorry," she said softly.

He looked over his shoulder. She was looking at him with her brows pulled together.

"I remember those days."

"How old are you?" he asked.

It was her turn to sigh. "Seventy-eight next month."

So, she was older than he. And was also as long lived as his kind. Meaning if they were to pursue anything…

Where the hell had that thought come from? There would be nothing to pursue. She was his charge. She would leave in a month's time.

"In case I don't see you then, happy birthday," he said. His heart squeezed but he kept his tone light.

He had done exactly as he'd promised and shown her the kindness and respect she deserved. They had formed a strange friendship, even if it felt forced at times. Like two people who had no choice but to share a life raft in the middle of the ocean.

She huffed a laugh. "Thanks."

They began their small talk as they did every day as he made her first meal of the day. They would discuss things like his duties as the guard, she would talk about the ways of her Clan, and then they would sit and eat together in silence.

It was the same thing every day.

He wanted to change things up, show her what she would miss if she chose to leave the security of Ahdlai.

"Let's eat in the garden today," he said.

He began to pack things in bags and containers he normally used for long treks through the woods during perimeter checks.

"Really?"

"Yeah. It's a nice day. The sun's out. It's a warm morning. No reason to stay locked in the house all day."

Her pretty face lit up, and he was happy he'd mentioned it.

"You don't mind carrying me again?"

"I'll only have to carry you to the pony." He loaded everything into a leather satchel. "You eventually need to name her."

Her dark blonde brows puckered. "I figured she had a name."

"She didn't belong to anyone. She has no name."

"Oh." Her lips formed a perfect O on that single word and Jhelan was suddenly fixated on her mouth.

He didn't know how long he stared at her mouth, how long he focused on her lips, but when she shifted in her seat and made a sound in her throat, he was snapped out of his lust filled stupor.

He had done so well at keeping his hands to himself, at keeping all thoughts of Claims and Bonds from his head in the two weeks she had been in his home. But watching her mouth form that simple word scattered all thoughts in his brain.

"Are we going? Or did you change your mind?"

Valdis's words snapped him back to reality. She was his charge, not a woman to be Claimed and filled with his seed.

"Yeah. Yes. Sorry. Daydreaming."

It wasn't a lie. He was daydreaming, only he would never tell her it involved tasting her lips.

Valdis sat atop the unnamed mare and watched Jhelan from the corner of her eye. They had formed a comfortable companionship, but he'd begun to act strangely over the past few days. He was still polite and no longer complained about being responsible for her, but he was more...

She couldn't think of the word. He stared at her more. His eyes flashed with iridescence during some of those times he watched her closely.

Was he once again growing resentful of her presence but was such a man of his word he wouldn't mention it?

That couldn't be it. Because she had caught him staring at her mouth before they'd left. Men only stared at a woman's lips for one reason.

And Valdis wasn't sure she would stop him if he were to move closer and kiss her.

Their companionship was bordering on attachment, but she knew the large part of it was due to her dependence on him. She even needed his help to use the toilet, and it had taken her days to rid herself of the humiliation that came each time.

Jhelan kept his hand wrapped around the lead while carrying a satchel over his other shoulder. And he said nothing to her as they traversed the large town of Ahdlai.

"How many people live here?"

He glanced back at her. "Last count was somewhere around six hundred. But the number changes with each birth."

"How many humans stayed after giving birth?"

He slowed so he could walk directly beside her instead of looking back to speak. "All of them. We offer additional protection if a mother chooses to return to her Clan, but none have left since. I think they like to stay close to their child."

"Even though they have no say in their upbringing?"

She was aware of the rules and laws of Ahdlai. It was one of the main reasons the humans in her Clan refused to breed for any paranormal beings. Even the ones who paid well or offered the perks Jhelan mentioned.

"They may visit their children. They're still a part of their lives, but no, they have no say in their upbringing. They become more of a…they become an extended family member, like an aunt or uncle."

"And you say we're stupid," she muttered under her breath.

Jhelan pulled the horse to a stop and turned to look up into Valdis's face. "I am sorry for what I said. Truly. I was tired. Angry. I don't think you're stupid. I think you're extremely intelligent and unbelievably strong."

She worried her bottom lip and searched his face. His expression didn't waver, his eyes didn't dart to the side. He looked as though he waited for her to forgive him.

"Thank you," she said.

That was the best she could say. She was confused, all mixed up inside. In a short time, she had gone from detesting this man's very presence and resenting the fact she relied on him to merely move from the bed to appreciating him and thinking of him as a friend.

Maybe more.

She was attracted to him. Had been since she had first looked into his crystalline blue eyes, since she'd seen his first genuine smile.

But it could go no further than that simple attraction. A mild crush. A touch of lust and infatuation.

"I'm forgiven for my own stupidity?"

Try as she might, she failed to hold back the smile and light chuckle that bubbled up in her chest. "Yes. You're forgiven for your stupidity."

He placed a hand over his heart and stumbled back a step, feigning shock.

Valdis reached down and tugged on the lead. "I really thought you were kind of a jerk," she admitted when he smiled up at her.

"I really thought you were kind of a pain in the ass," he shot back.

They stared at each other straight faced for a few heartbeats before they both broke into laughter.

"I am a pain in the ass."

"And I really am a jerk," Jhelan said, tugging on the lead to get the pony moving.

People waved or smiled as Jhelan and Valdis passed. They all truly did appear happy in Ahdlai. And she had zero doubt they were safe, not with men like Jhelan guarding them.

The garden was bustling with life as people tended to the blooms coming to life in the late spring morning. Birds chirped in nearby trees. The sounds of children laughing came from somewhere near the back of the large Palace.

The sound grew louder as a parade of young boys and girls rounded the corner in two lines, an Elven woman leading the way. One of the little girls looked directly at Valdis and smiled. The girl couldn't have been more than three or four years old.

As the others continued on their way, the girl broke from the group, plucked a flower from the garden, and ran on her wobbly legs to where Valdis sat atop the mare.

"Hi," she said, her little voice so sweet.

"Hi, there," Valdis said. As the girl stood on her toes to hand the flower over, Valdis took it between her fingers and smiled. "Thank you so much. I'm Valdis. What's your name?"

"Flora," the girl answered.

"Stay in line, sweetheart," the woman called.

Valdis didn't know whether the woman was a teacher, some form of childcare, or a trainer of some form. But she didn't look stern nor angry that little Flora had left the line to interact with the newcomer to Ahdlai.

"Bye," Flora said, then surprised Valdis when she hugged Valdis's leg like she was hugging her around the neck.

All she could do from where she sat was stroke the little girl's head.

Little Flora ran back to the group of children, looking back with a hearty wave when she was back in her place in line then followed along as they all headed inside the Palace.

It truly was a beautifully perfect day. Fluffy clouds shielded the sun periodically, a light breeze carried the scent of the forest that surrounded the town. It was peaceful here. And little Flora had made the day even better.

While she'd been happy with her Clan, she had never truly rested, had never been able to relax. There was always some job to be done for the mere survival of her people. They were always on edge, waiting for the next attack or the next bout of sickness or starvation when the winter months offered less food.

The women in this town had rounded bodies, their hips were full, their skin healthy and soft. The children appeared happy and so well cared for. And everyone she had come near had smelled of flowers or citrus fruit.

Without thinking, Valdis lifted an arm and sniffed her forearm.

"What are you doing?"

"What do I smell like?" she asked, holding her arm out to him.

He looked at her as if she'd grown a third eye.

"What?"

"Everyone smells like flowers or citrus. What do I smell like?"

"You use what I have in my bathroom. Do you really think I would use something that smelled like a woman?"

He gripped her hips and helped her from the pony, his hands firm and warm. And when he settled her on a bench near a table, she found she missed his touch when he pulled away.

Damn it. These were not feelings she wanted, not now, not with this man, not when her heart was still a complete and total mess.

She grieved the loss of her Clan, but Jhelan's presence made it a tiny bit better. Each time sorrow began to drown her, Jhelan seemed to know and would say or do just the right thing to bring a smile to her face or comfort her enough to go on with her day.

"So, I smell like citrus," Valdis said, lifting her arm to her nose again.

Jhelan shook his head as he placed the food on the table. "You realize you're sniffing yourself, right? People already think you're strange."

She stopped and frowned at him. "They think I'm strange?"

"No. But I got you to stop smelling your arm."

Shaking her head, she rolled her eyes and accepted the servings of food he handed to her, contained in bowls so unlike the fancy ones they used when they dined with the Royal Family and the guard.

"Tell me about your job. I want to know more."

"What's there to know?" he asked.

He settled himself beside her instead of across the table. It was awkward to talk if they wanted to look at each other, but they both had an amazing view of the fountain from this position. And she really enjoyed the way she felt when he was near.

Perhaps she had empathic abilities, because she could have sworn she felt his emotions when he touched her. Or she could simply be projecting her own. Being an empath wouldn't have been the gift she would have chosen, but it was better than having none.

Then again, she didn't recall feeling anything from Ihsander the one time he had carried her, or the healer each time she tended to Valdis's healing injuries.

"There's not much to tell, really. I keep the Royal Family safe. I keep the residents of Ahdlai safe. I ensure the *Ihllr* or any other enemies stay away from our territory. That's it."

"But you seem like you love it."

"It's all I've ever known."

"You were raised as a guard member?"

Jhelan rolled his neck; it cracked in a series of pops. "My father was a guard member. My mother was…she was a lot like you."

"How so?"

"She was a fighter. A warrior. She lived within the forest before she mated with my father. Led a rather large Clan, kept them safe without the aid of anyone from Ahdlai. I think that's why my dad chose her."

Valdis chewed and swallowed, then sipped water from the canteen she shared with Jhelan.

"Was it against your mother's will? The Claim?"

She didn't want to ask that question, didn't want to know the answer, but it was out of her mouth before she could suck it back down her throat.

"No. Her Clan had been attacked by local Shape-Shifters. They had lost a few of their members and she knew mating with a guard member would offer another layer of protection."

She turned to look at his profile. "Did she stay in town?"

A smile slowly stretched on his face. "Every single member of the Clan moved into town. They were the first large settlement welcomed in after Arkyn's parents took control of the region."

"Your mom is still here?"

The smile slowly bled from his face. "She joined the guard. She was the first and only female of any species to be a member of the Royal guard."

Her brows shot up her forehead as she stared wide eyed at Jhelan. "Seriously? Your mom went out and did what you guys do?"

"There were less people to protect back then, but yeah. She was only a couple inches shorter than me. And commanded respect from everyone she met."

Was. He referred to his mom in past tense, meaning she was no longer living.

"Why do you say she was like me?"

He huffed a laugh and took a big bite from his sandwich. "She was feisty as hell. And refused to ask for help from anyone. She would rather break her back than ask Dad or anyone else to help carry something that was twice her size."

"You're saying we're both stubborn."

He pointed his sandwich toward her. "That, too."

Valdis chuckled and went back to her breakfast.

People continued to pass by, smiling or nodding their greeting. Another little girl lifted her hand and waved heartily at Valdis. Valdis waved back with a wide grin.

"Do you want to have dinner in the dining hall or back at home tonight?" Jhelan asked.

Back at home. It had been her home for two weeks, yet she still didn't fully feel as though she belonged there. It would take far longer for her heart to leave the freedom of the forest and be content behind walls again. But how wonderful would it be to never have to wonder where her next meal would come from or whether she would eat that day?

How wonderful would it be to be able to lay her head down at night and sleep without waking at every sound, wondering if another group had tracked her Clan and was there to steal away the women and kill the men?

What was she doing? Sitting in the garden, she was picturing her future in Ahdlai. More than that – she was picturing her future with Jhelan.

They had formed a comfortable existence together. Nothing more. He would be happy when she was no longer his burden, when he no longer had to heft her from one location to the other, when he no longer had to cook her meals or help her to the bathroom.

He had been kind to her, but he had been ordered by the prince to care for her while she healed.

The bruising was gone. The stitches had been removed. But her foot still ached and she was still unable to put her weight on it. She sometimes dreamed of running, of putting both feet on the ground and taking off at a sprint.

It would be another few weeks before her right leg was strong again after so much time of disuse.

"We can eat at your place," she said, refusing to use the word *home*.

She loved eating in the Palace, loved the desserts provided after the meal, but she didn't want to get any closer to the people here than she already had. She had a few weeks left, maybe a little over a month.

She needed to prepare her heart to leave. She had to forbid herself from growing attached to any single member of this town.

Even Jhelan.

It didn't matter how kind he had been. It didn't matter that his gentle caresses along her scars sent tingles all the way to her toes. It didn't matter that she'd begun to look forward to when he would lift her into his arms so she could feel his body against hers.

He wasn't hers. He would never be hers.

She was alone. Again. She would not allow herself to feel anything more than gratitude toward Jhelan only to have him taken from her when she walked away.

Or worse. He could be killed on duty when he was done with his role as her sole caregiver.

"What's wrong?" he asked.

She frowned up at him, then quickly schooled her face. "Nothing. Daydreaming."

His lips twitched. He had caught on that she'd used the same wording he had when he'd stared at her mouth.

Could he possibly feel for her more than she believed? Could he feel more for her than simple lust or the need to sire an heir, to continue his bloodline?

"We have all day. And I really don't feel like sitting in the house. Feel like exploring the Palace grounds? You've only seen the town and the garden. We can stay within the walls if being out there scares you."

"I lived *out there* my whole life," she said.

"You weren't incapacitated then. We can bring Ihsander and Ahdeben if you'll feel safer. I'm sure Ahrkyn wouldn't mind tagging along, too. And I haven't been outside the walls in a while."

Since Valdis's arrival.

"We can really go into the forest? We can wander the woods?"

"Is that what you want?"

Her heart raced and a smile stretched wide on her face. "So much."

She'd missed it. She had missed the smell of the leaves that had fallen to rot on the ground, the scent of pine, the sounds of animals scurrying about.

"Then it's done. We'll track down the others, pack a satchel with some snacks, and we'll wander through the woods for a few hours. I'll even let you pretend you're a member of the guard."

Valdis frowned. "What?"

His cheeks turned pink as he looked away and rubbed the back of the neck. "I'll want you to at least wear one of our battle vests. Just in case."

"Ah. I'll get to *pretend* I'm a guard member."

He gave her a sheepish smile. Valdis couldn't hold back. A giggle bubbled up her chest and burst from her mouth.

"You want me to dress like you guys for protection, but you thought wording it that way would make me feel better. I was wrong. You're not a jerk. You're kind of a weirdo."

Jhelan nudged her with his shoulder and stood to clean up their mess.

He then helped her onto the pony and they were off to track down his friends so they could take Valdis into the woods.

Back to her true home.

Chapter Seven

The look on Valdis's face when he suggested heading outside of the walls to wander through the woods nearly broke Jhelan's heart.

He was happy she was happy. Of course he was. But he wanted her to be as happy here in the center of Ahdlai. With him.

Jhelan had truly believed he wanted nothing to do with Claiming or mating a female. And he truly had no desire to be Bonded to one for life.

Yet, the moment he let his guard down and saw her for who she was rather than a burden or hassle, his heart began to warm toward her. His body hardened any time she was pressed against his chest as he carried her or even with the lightest touch of her fingers. His body reacted any time he was near her. There was nothing he could do about it. She was a beautiful woman.

And her beauty was far more than simply skin deep.

He had watched as she lit up any time someone smiled her way or greeted her. She had even warmed up to his buddies. And they liked her. They no longer winced when she cursed or gave them grief.

In reality, they'd begun to treat her as one of them instead of a woman who had come to them in deep need of medical care and hot meals.

They didn't have to say the words for Jhelan to know they were as reluctant to see her go as him.

Well, maybe not quite as much as he.

Now, Jhelan and Valdis wandered past the last row of houses, Valdis atop the pony she had yet to name, two men on either side of her and two following closely behind as though she were the Queen of Ahdlai. The prince demanded he stay near the side opposite of Jhelan, his eyes watchful, his body ready for any form of surprise attack.

It was rare for their enemies to come so close to the town and especially the Palace. But it wasn't out of the question. The guard stayed ready for anything at all times.

"I hope you brought enough food for all of us," Ihsander teased.

"Who said I'm sharing?" Valdis teased back.

The two had formed a fairly close friendship. But Ihsander, like the others, could sense the attachment Jhelan had formed to the woman and kept his distance, only touching her when absolutely necessary.

The party of five continued until they were well over a mile from town. Jhelan watched Valdis's face, watched as her body relaxed and her eyes filled with joy.

This was her home. This was all she had known her whole life. She'd grown comfortable with her life in Ahdlai and appeared content there.

But here? She truly seemed happy. She was free.

"Do you want to get down? I packed a pelt. We can spread it out and enjoy the fresh air," Jhelan offered.

"Yay! Picnic time," Ihsander said with a grin.

"You know, I thought Jhelan was a weirdo. I think you might very well be more so," Valdis said.

The men chuckled.

Jhelan slowed the horse to a standstill and wrapped the lead around a small tree. Then, like every single time he touched her, his heart thumped madly in his chest as he gripped her small waist and lowered her until he could pull her against his chest and cradle her in his arms.

He loved these moments, as fleeting as they were. He loved the weight of her body, loved the feel of her against his chest, loved the way she draped one arm around his neck and leaned into him.

Pretending to seek the perfect spot, he held her a little longer. He would do nearly anything to have her in his arms by her own accord. He would give his left foot to have her want his hands on her, his body lined along hers, his weight pressing her down into the mattress.

Valdis's head turned and she looked into his face. There was a smile there, both on her lips and in her eyes, the kind of smile that told him she knew exactly what he was doing.

She surprised the hell out of him when she snuggled against him a little more and tightened the arm she had around his neck.

Perhaps she did feel something more for him than gratitude, saw him as more than a simple companion.

Or perhaps he was hoping for more, hoping he was enough to keep her in Ahdlai long after her foot was healed and the binding was removed.

He couldn't continue to walk around in circles, so he picked a spot and set her down. Ihsander had carried the satchel containing the meager snacks and pelt Jhelan packed for their trip, laying everything near Valdis.

Once everyone was settled, Valdis leaned against the tree at her back and closed her eyes, inhaling deeply before crossing her good ankle over the other.

"This is perfect," she muttered just above a whisper.

A breeze ruffled her honey-colored hair, blowing a strand across her face. Jhelan couldn't help himself. He reached forward and moved the hair away, tucking it behind her ear.

Valdis's lids slowly lifted and she smiled at him. "Thanks."

"Snacks," Ihsander said, ruining the moment.

With a chuckle, Valdis grabbed the satchel by its strap and tossed it toward Ihsander.

"I swear you guys are always hungry. You wouldn't survive a week in the forest."

"Why do you choose to live out here?" Ahdeben asked. He looked around. "There is nothing. No food. No shelter."

"There's food and shelter if you look for it."

Valdis tilted her head back and squinted her eyes. Then lifted a hand and pointed. "See that nest? If you check at the right time, there will be eggs. If you find a river or lake, there are fish. And, if you're as amazing as I am, you can hunt for bigger game."

"There isn't much of that left behind after the war," Ahdeben said.

Valdis shook her head. "No. But if you can steal chickens or other livestock from the different towns, you can breed your own livestock. If you can steal the right kind of vegetable or fruit from someone else's garden, you can harvest the seeds and grow your own garden. At least until you're found and have to move on."

"Your Clan steals from the towns?" Prince Ahrkyn asked.

There wasn't the least bit of guilt on her face. "We do what we have to to survive and feed any children who are born among the humans."

"Then I have to ask again, why would anyone choose to live out here rather than within the safety of Ahdlai?" Ahdeben asked.

Her shoulders rose and fell. "It's all I've ever known. I was young when my parents were murdered. I learned to survive out here, then joined my first Clan. It's a freedom you don't get when you live under someone else's laws and rules."

"Those laws and rules are there to protect everyone, including the humans," Ahrkyn said.

"It's hard to see it that way when the humans volunteer to carry your child for the extra protection and small amount of food gifted to them only to never see their son or daughter again."

"You know they're allowed to stay in town. They're given homes of their own. I already told you that," Jhelan said.

"And the mother has no say in how her child is raised, and is treated like a distant relative rather than the person who grew the child within her own body."

"But you don't risk that. You can't breed with anyone else, either. Why not find a town of Fae?" Ahrkyn asked.

She had finally opened up about her lineage to the men, but only the four who sat with her now.

"I grew up with humans. The only Fae I ever knew died before they could teach me a single thing about my heritage. And I have no gifts, no magic. How well do you think I would be accepted into a Court with nothing to offer? I know you all know the history of my people. They're not exactly loving and kind. They wouldn't take me in simply because I'm an orphan."

That answer appeased Ahdeben's curiosity. And gave Jhelan yet another glimpse into the layers that made up Valdis.

The group enjoyed the weather, enjoyed the early spring's warmth, enjoyed each other's company. Jhelan had a hard time keeping his eyes from Valdis, even when she would catch him staring at her.

But she no longer asked why he was staring, only smiled or winked at him.

And gave him more hope than someone like him should have.

A sense of alarm perked up Jhelan's senses.

"Can you pass me –"

Ahrkyn threw up a hand, silencing Valdis. She opened her mouth, probably to tell him exactly what she thought of being shushed, but noticed the deep frown drawing his brows low and the intensity on his face.

A half second later, Jhelan, Ihsander, and Ahdeben caught the scent. There was someone nearby. More than one. And they didn't carry the scent of the Elves or humans of Ahdlai.

The group could wait to determine if the trespassers were nearly passing by or simply an ally visiting the region.

But not with Valdis unable to defend herself should the men have to split up. And if one was left behind to watch over her, the others could be outnumbered. Or Jhelan – because he would be the one to watch over her for more reasons than Ahrkyn's declaration that he was responsible for her – could be outnumbered if this was some form of sneak attack or ambush.

With a jerk of his head, Ahrkyn made the decision for them. They would head back to the town, stash Valdis somewhere safe, then investigate with a few more members of the guard. Just because the four of them had battled great numbers didn't mean they wanted to again. They always returned with a slew of injuries and had to be sidelined while they healed.

"Can you truly ride?" Jhelan whispered in Valdis's ear.

She pulled back, fire bright in her mossy eyes as she nodded. She might not have been able to detect the trespassers, but she could sense the tension rolling from the men around her.

Leaning forward again, his lips brushed against her ear. "If I say so, kick that horse as hard as you can and head straight for the Palace. Don't stop at the houses. Go straight to the gate. They'll let you in immediately."

She turned her head until her mouth was near his ear.

"What about you?"

Jhelan smiled at both the possibility of a fight and the concern he heard in her breathy words.

Pulling back to look into her eyes, he let her see his grin. "This is my favorite part of the job," he whispered.

She was breathing heavily, her eyes were wide, but her jaw was set in a determined line, and she squared her shoulders as he lifted her quickly and set her on the horse.

The trip back to the town surrounding Ahdlai was at a faster clip. The men spread around Valdis further, Jhelan and Ahrkyn in the front, and Ahdeben and Ihsander bringing up the rear.

Their eyes constantly moved, their ears were tuned to any nearby sounds, their senses open as they waited to feel the familiar prickle of a paranormal being closing in on them.

Valdis kept control of the lead of the pony, her legs on either side of the animal, and she looked as vigilant and ready for battle as the men.

So much like his mother. So ready to fight, to protect herself and those whom she cared for most.

The moment the houses came into view, the group as one began to jog until they were at the gate.

"Open up. Let her in and keep an eye on her," Jhelan said.

He smacked the pony on the rear when there was enough space for the small beast to get inside the walls.

Valdis turned and looked over her shoulder. "Be careful," she yelled just before the gate closed, cutting off his view of a woman he prayed he would once again have in his arms.

The gates closed behind her, and Valdis's heart hammered like crazy behind her ribs. She had no idea who or what the men detected, but it was enough for them to rush her back to the safety of the Palace walls instead of leaving her inside of Jhelan's house.

Guard members ran past her, the leather of their battle gear creaking, their hands gripped around the handles of swords.

"What is it? What's happening?" the King asked from the lawn as he rushed toward Valdis.

"I don't know. The men tensed then rushed me back here. They behaved as though there was a threat."

King Nhaeem looked thoughtful as he watched the men he'd hired to protect his people flood through the gate, running straight toward possible danger.

"They'll handle it. My son and his friends are the best of Ahdlai."

The King glanced up at Valdis, then did a double take.

"Don't worry, girl. They'll be fine. And we'll keep you safe until Jhelan returns for you."

He took the lead from Valdis's hand and led the pony to the front step, then removed her from the animal without asking and carried her inside.

"Have you grown weary of being toted around like a toddler?" he asked as he lowered her onto a chair.

"I was tired of it from day one," she said, forcing a smile she knew didn't reach her eyes.

Valdis lifted a hand and chewed her thumbnail. She had fought against forming an attachment in her time here, yet she had failed. She had grown attached to Ihsander, to Ahdeben and Ahrkyn.

And she was extremely attached to Jhelan.

She had fought against forming a connection and lost. He held her heart, whether she ever had the opportunity to tell him. In the weeks they'd spent together, he had embedded himself so deeply in every cell of her body that she wasn't sure she would ever forget him should she choose to return to the forest.

Did she wish to return? Did she want to once again scrounge for food, for supplies, for shelter and heat? Did she want to roam the world alone again? Or to pray she found another group of people willing to take her in based on what she could contribute to their Clan?

Or did she wish to stay with Jhelan, with the people of Ahdlai who had treated her as though she were already a member, who had not once asked what she could give in return for her stay or the medical treatment she received from the healer.

People hurried around, nodding at her as they passed, asking if she needed anything while she waited.

Elabeth, one of the staff she had seen at every meal they ate in the Palace, stopped beside her. "Are you comfortable here? Would you rather wait on the couch? Or I can have someone take you to the dining room for something to eat."

Her appetite would not return until she saw Jhelan's face, until she saw with her own eyes that he was alive and well.

"I'm fine here. Thank you."

Valdis was within sight of the front door. She would prefer to wait outside so she would see the moment Jhelan sauntered back through the gate. But if the King felt she was safer inside the Palace, she would defer to him. This was his region, his territory, and his home. She was merely a guest.

Valdis had never been one to sit around and wait, to let others fight while she hid. Yet, here she was, unable to do anything more than what she hated most – waiting.

Voices rose outside. Bodies hurried past her and through the front door, slamming it shut in their haste.

Then the King and Queen walked at a fast clip to head the same way as everyone else, and Valdis continued to sit in the seat where the King had deposited her. Waiting. Waiting to discover whether Ahdlai was in danger, waiting to discover whether the guard was engaged in battle…

Waiting to discover whether she would see Jhelan's hypnotic cerulean eyes again. If she would ever feel his arms wrapped around her as he carried her so carefully, as if she were a precious package.

He no longer made her feel as though he were forced to tend to her, but rather he enjoyed it. She no longer felt as though she were forced to stay within in his home, but began to dread the day when she had to decide whether to stay or leave.

Seconds turned into minutes and Valdis's nerves were frayed. Patience had never been one of her stronger virtues, never something she had quite mastered.

Nope. She couldn't wait any longer. *Wouldn't* wait any longer.

Pushing to the edge of the chair, she gingerly placed her broken foot on the ground. This would be the first time she attempted to put any weight on the shattered bones. But she had to know, had to see for herself what future lie ahead for her.

One slow, painful step at a time, she hobbled her way to the door, intent on at least getting to the stoop. Her bones might have still been healing, but she wasn't in agony, partly from adrenaline, but mostly from pure determination.

She hated that she had been whisked away when facing danger. She hated that she was relying on others for her protection when, given a weapon, she could fight alongside Jhelan. She could help protect Ahdlai. She could watch Jhelan's back.

As each step jarred her healing foot, she made up her mind then and there – if he wanted her, if Jhelan asked her to stay, she would. She would remain in Ahdlai, continue to sleep in his house, and continue to sleep in his bed.

But only if he would lie beside her each night.

Chapter Eight

Jhelan, Ihsander, Ahdeben, and Ahrkyn escorted the newcomers to the gate and onto the Palace lawn.

He didn't regret returning Valdis to the care of the guards behind the walls. Since he had no idea who was approaching, he refused to risk her being hurt, taken, or killed when there were others who would keep her safe without a second thought.

It was the job of the guard to maintain peace and provide protection for all those who resided within the territory and the region. She was as much a member as anyone else for as long as she stayed within the town.

Hell, he knew he would continue to protect her from afar if she chose to return to the harsh life of the wilderness. He would walk with her, hand and hand, into the unknown if she would have him.

"What is this?" the King called as he walked across the large expanse of lawn leading from the front steps of the Palace to where the guard escorted three people.

"They have brought a warning," Prince Ahrkyn called to his father.

The King instantly tensed and a flash of light entered his eyes, indicating his heightened emotion.

"Are they a threat to my people?"

"We are not, Your Highness," an ogre standing at least seven feet tall said with a bow. "We are here to bring a warning as we have heard…things being whispered throughout the many groups we have come across."

"And what warning is that?"

"You will soon be under attack. The *Ihllr* have been recruiting and will lay siege to your region. They plan to slay every member of the Royal Family and any who refuse to bend the knee to their leader."

"What is your name?" King Nhaeem asked.

"I am called Brizio of Ahde, Your Highness."

The King tilted his head and looked the ogre from head to toe.

"You are a long way from home, Brizio."

"I travel with a Coven of witches. I am what some may call a wanderer, though I prefer to think of myself as an explorer."

"Welcome. You and your companions may join us within the Palace. We have much to discuss. But I will warn you, should you or your magical friends plan to deceive myself or any of my guard, we have gifts of our own to use against anything you might throw at us."

"Understood, Your Highness."

The guard not presently watching the perimeter or standing guard in the watchtowers escorted Brizio and his companions across the lawn.

Jhelan glanced at the stoop then did a double take. Valdis was leaning against a column propping the covering. She breathed heavily, her face was flushed from exertion, and there was no one nearby who could have carried her.

What was she thinking? She could have so easily caused permanent damage to her foot or fallen and injured herself again.

"Excuse me, Your Highness," Jhelan said to Ahrkyn, using the formal title in front of the strangers.

Ahrkyn frowned at him, looked in the direction Jhelan stared, then nodded. "Go."

Moving away from the grouping of men, Jhelan jogged to where Valdis waited.

"What are you doing?"

"What happened? Are you okay? Is Ahdlai under attack?"

Her eyes roamed his body frantically, then settled on his face, a look of relief plain in her beautiful eyes.

"We are not under attack. But one is imminent. Why are you out here? Why did you not wait for someone to carry you? I told you I would return."

"I...I had to see for myself. And I couldn't wait any longer for news. I hate waiting. Especially if I have to wait to discover the fate of —"

She cut herself off before she could say anymore, sucking her lips into her mouth as though to trap the words before they could pour forth.

He lifted her into his arms, earning a squeak with his speed, and hurried her through the front door and out of sight of the newcomers. He didn't fear they would attack her, but wanted to speak with her without prying eyes or ears. Down the hallway, through the living area, through the door and onto the patio that overlooked the lawn stretching over an acre along the back of the Palace property.

Jhelan didn't settle her on a chair, but lowered onto one himself, keeping her wrapped in his arms.

"I was so afraid," he confessed.

"Then why didn't you wait to find more guard members to investigate?"

He frowned at her as a smile tugged at his lips. "I wasn't afraid for myself, *khaere*, but for you. You're in no condition to fight. Had there been a threat out there, more than the four of us could have handled, you could have been hurt. Or taken. Or killed. I couldn't live with any of those options."

He cupped her face in one hand and took a chance. He leaned forward, desperate to finally feel the lips he'd been so fixated on. Even if only once.

There was no hesitation when she, too, leaned forward and closed the distance between them. The moment their lips touched it was as if fire ignited within him, sending heat through his veins and to every limb. He had never felt such intensity with such a simple touch. He had never felt as though the world had simply faded away by having a woman in his arms.

He had never felt for anything or anyone the way he felt for Valdis.

They didn't deepen the kiss, but her arms snaked around his neck as she pulled herself closer to his body until her full breasts were mashed against his chest. She had put on some healthy weight in the weeks she'd been in Ahdlai. She had been beautiful as she was, injuries and all. Now that she was no longer emaciated, she was worthy of being immortalized by a painting or statue.

At least in his head.

When Valdis finally pulled back, there was a hint of light in her beautiful Fae eyes. Instead of the glow in the irises as his kind possessed, her glow came directly from her dilated pupils.

"I was so scared, Jhelan. I tried. I tried so hard not to get attached to you. I didn't want to get attached to you. To anyone. I didn't want to care for someone again and have them ripped away. Then you rushed me back here and I didn't know what was happening, if you were engaged in battle, if you had been killed."

"So, you hobbled outside to see me with your own eyes."

"Yes."

Warmth spread from his heart through his chest. He smiled. "So damn stubborn," he muttered, before leaning forward to feather a kiss across her lips again.

She started hard and hissed in a breath.

Pulling away, she darted a look at her arm the same time he felt the tingling sensation growing up his own.

As he watched in absolute astonishment, matching brands grew along their arms. He knew, were they topless, the brands would grow up their biceps and over their shoulders. They had managed to complete the Bond with nothing more than acknowledging their feelings for each other and a kiss. Others had gone through far more, had spent months or years together, had made love before their Bond completed.

But Mother Universe was adamant there was no other for either of them.

They were now bound in the most profound way. It was irreversible. Whether either of them ever made the decision to walk away, they would merely be pulled right back together.

The high point of this Bond was no matter where Valdis went in the world, Jhelan could find her. Should some asshole decide to steal her away from him, Jhelan could track her through that Bond.

He could also now feel her emotions as though they were his own.

She was confused, appalled, ecstatic…

And she loved him.

That last one nearly caused tears to build in Jhelan's eyes. But he was a warrior. A member of the Royal guard. Warriors did not shed a tear.

They could, however, taste their new mate's lips again and make plans to solidify the Bond the moment they were behind closed doors.

Valdis went back and forth between craving more of Jhelan's touch to staring at her arm. She was not Elven, yet the Universe had marked her with the Bonding brand of their kind. She had not truly been given a choice as to who her life mate would be, whether she would have the choice to walk away when the time came.

Although she had already made up her mind to stay by Jhelan's side if he would have her, she wasn't keen on the idea that she was no longer in charge of her own destiny.

But none of that mattered. Not now. Not at this moment. All that mattered was the sense of rightness that flooded her senses and sent fire through her veins. Each time his lips touched hers it felt like lightning exploded from within her, as if at any moment she would go insane if she didn't have him closer, if she didn't feel his skin on hers, if she didn't feel him inside of her.

Never in her life had she desired a man as much as she did Jhelan. Never in her life had she found a man whom she wanted to Claim her…in more ways than one.

Unfortunately, there was something going on within the region. Otherwise, three strangers wouldn't have been escorted within the walls by a large contingency of guards.

"Who was with you? Who is here?" she asked.

He groaned as he pulled back and dropped against the seat. "They've come to warn us. Apparently, the *Ihllr* is planning something big. And they're recruiting others. That's all the information I was able to get before my eyes landed on you."

Her body tingled and she felt a girly sigh build in her chest.

"I didn't mean to distract you."

He grunted. "You've been nothing but a distraction from day one, *khaere*."

That was the second time he had called her that. And by the way he used it, she assumed it was an Elven term of endearment. And really liked the way it sounded on his lips.

"Do you want me to wait at your house while you speak with the King and Queen? Or I can hang out here."

"I want you at my side."

She frowned. "I highly doubt the King will want an outsider listening in on any strategies for an upcoming battle."

His frown mirrored her own. "You are not an outsider, *khaere*. Not anymore." He held his arm against hers. "You are now bound to me. You are bound to me in a way so few are blessed to experience. The King will understand my need to be near you. He already experienced it with Queen Ahlmeda. You have seen their marks. They appear as silvery lines, almost like faded scars."

"Why are their marks so faint?"

"Ours will be to any others, as well. They'll only see faint silver designs where only you and I will be able to trace the true patterns and eventually learn their meanings."

"Your world is so different than the one I've always known."

He huffed a laugh. "The Fae world isn't exactly normal. You've just never been privy to their mating rituals. But that's for another time. As much as I want to carry you to *our* home," he said, emphasizing the word 'our', "I still have a duty to protect Ahdlai and its residents."

He stood with her cradled to his chest and followed the sounds of raised masculine voices.

A large number of men crowded around the table. Some sat, including the King and prince, while others stood nearby, shouting their opinion, doing their best to be heard over the noise.

Jhelan deposited Valdis in a chair off to the side where she was safe from the throng of bodies, but close enough he could reach out to touch her.

Several sets of eyes darted her way, noticed her arm, then quickly looked away in a show of respect to Jhelan and Valdis as well as the Bond.

She knew so little about what she was now being thrust into, knew so little about the Elven ways. But for the first time in as long as she could remember, she felt she was exactly where she was meant to be.

"We must meet them somewhere far from Ahdlai," a male yelled.

"We cannot cross the boundary into Mhazin. That will surely be seen as an act of war," another yelled.

"They must not be allowed near our town. We can fight them in the woods, meet them before they get too close," yet another male called out.

"How could we do that? We know nothing of the forest short of our perimeter checks. As far as we know, they may have recruited Shape-Shifters or even the humans who live among the wilderness."

Over and over, males yelled their opinions as the King and prince listened, pensive looks on both handsome faces.

"I know the forest well," Valdis said.

They continued to yell, continued to ignore her presence.

"I said I know the forest well. I know where every cave is, where every stream runs, where the best and worst places for battle would be," she said, raising her voice to be heard.

Slowly, conversation began to slow and, one by one, they each looked in her direction.

"There is a reason so many have been able to survive without the aid of any help from the Palace. We knew where to hide, knew which trees offered the best coverage, knew where wild berries grew."

"You were captured. Your people were slaughtered," Ihsander reminded her, his tone gentle.

Pain lanced her heart. Pushing the emotion away, she raised her chin and looked at each man in turn. "We were found. But we also survived long before that. I, personally, survived among the trees for the first sixty-three years of my life."

The prince raised one brow at her. "What are you offering, Valdis?"

"I can guide you to the best areas to lay a trap. I can show you where to avoid. I can show you where to hide large numbers of guard to remain undetected until the *Ihllr* is close enough."

"No," Jhelan said.

She shot him a look. "Excuse me?"

"No. You are still healing. You cannot—"

"I have Little Dove. I can ride her through the woods. With all of you, there will be no risk to me. And I hate to break it to you big, strong men, but I'm very good with a sword and very good with a bow and arrow. Give me a weapon, put me atop my pony, and I can guide you."

Jhelan's lips twitched, and he muttered, "Little Dove? Of all names, that's what you've chosen?"

She shrugged up one shoulder. "It was stuck in my head. She's as white as a dove and so much smaller than the steeds and other mares."

His body shook with a contained chuckle.

The men looked to the King and waited to hear his opinion.

"How vast of an area have you traveled?"

"I've been to both borders, north and south, although I have not been far to the east. There isn't much left there to scavenge and the land isn't fertile enough for crops."

King Nhaeem nodded slowly then silently convened with his son.

"If there were enough men, she would not be in danger," Prince Ahrkyn said.

"I said no," Jhelan said.

Valdis reached forward and grabbed his hand. When he turned his head to look down at her, she shot him a saccharine sweet smile. "I know we don't know each other all that well yet but you'll have to learn to forget all about that word when it comes to me. I don't ask permission for anything. And I won't be told what I can and can't do."

Jhelan lowered to his knees in front of her, his back to the rest of the room.

Conversation slowly grew as they gave the newly Bonded couple a modicum of privacy.

"I do not say that because I don't believe you're capable. We have no idea how far along the *Ihllr* are in their planning. They could be headed here now. Should they bring a large enough number to overrun the guard we bring along, there would be nothing we could do to protect you. And I would rather run a dagger across my own throat than risk your safety."

He clasped the hand with the design flowing down to her fingertips. Palm to palm, her Bonding mark throbbed, but in a pleasurable way and she wondered if his did, too. She struggled to discern where she ended and he began, whether the feelings of possessiveness were his or her own.

And wondered whether the new wave of affection causing her heart to warm was simply a combination of their emotions swelling within her.

"Send out a scouting party. Ensure the enemy isn't nearby. Then I'll ride out with you all and show you. I can help. Let me help."

It was all she could do for now. Until she was able to walk on her own two feet, she would be no good in hand-to-hand combat.

But this? This she could do. She could help them form a strategy, show them the places that would take them straight into an ambush, show them the places where they would have the high ground.

"We have some of the brightest minds within Ahdlai. If no one can find a better plan, than I will concede. But only if you're fully geared up and only if you do what I say when I say," Jhelan said.

"Did I not listen to you earlier when you told me to head for the Palace at your word?"

"You never had to run. So I don't know if you would have listened or not," he pointed out.

There was a beat where they tried their best to glare at each other, both unwilling to compromise, but it lasted only a few seconds before they smiled and leaned forward. As it had each time, Valdis's body felt like it would burst into flames at the first contact of Jhelan's lips.

Someone cleared their throat, an obvious sign for Jhelan to return to his duties.

He sighed heavily and pushed to his feet. Even as he moved closer to the table, he never strayed so far that she couldn't simply reach out and touch him. The desire to touch him as much as possible was strong. And she could feel that same urge pouring from him.

She had fought being Claimed by a man her whole life. Had strayed as far from the non-humans, even her own kind, since entering the forest.

And now she couldn't imagine going another second without Jhelan by her side.

She had become possessed, possessed by the man who stole glances at her, possessed by the man who had tended to her injuries, cooked every meal for her, and carried her anywhere she needed to go. She had become possessed by the man who found her a means to traverse the wilderness for no other reason than to make her happy, who had given up his bed so she would be comfortable, had learned to cook so she would grow stronger.

Yeah. She was in way over her head and completely, irrevocably attached to Jhelan. And she could no longer find the downside in that.

Chapter Nine

He needed to leave the Palace. He needed to lift Valdis into his arms, rush to his home, and lay her on his bed. And then he needed to run his hands across every inch of her.

He had barely seen her body once and that was in the beginning when he saw her as a collar around his throat, something that kept him tethered to the town and prevented him from doing his job.

What an idiot. He'd had an opportunity and had blown it.

Never again.

The moment Jhelan had Valdis in his bed and under his hands, he would touch, kiss, and lick every part of her starting at her toes. He wouldn't stop until she squirmed and begged for more.

He –

"Jhelan, would you be amenable to that?" Prince Ahrkyn asked.

Jhelan blinked a few times and shook his head.

Oh no. They had been discussing battle plans and he was fantasizing about burying himself in his mate's warm, tight body.

"I'm sorry, Your Highness," Jhelan said. Ahrkyn rolled his eyes, his head turned so the newcomers wouldn't see. "I was deep in thought about Valdis's plan. Have you come up with a better strategy?"

Ahrkyn better say yes, because Jhelan refused to take Valdis out there, regardless of what he'd told her.

Excitement caused his heart to race. Then he realized it wasn't his own. He was feeling Valdis's emotions as well as his own. Had she felt the lust that had caused him to forget his place as head of the guard and tune out the rest of the room?

He couldn't turn to look at her, couldn't dwell on the scent of her arousal.

Yeah. She'd felt his lust.

"That was exactly what we were discussing. For now, it seems the best plan. I will send a contingency of scouts in different directions to ensure there are no *Ihllr* or spies. If they declare it safe, we will leave enough behind to ensure the safety of the Palace and town and the rest of the guard will go with us."

Jhelan opened his mouth to argue, something he really shouldn't do in front of the ogre and witches. Jhelan and Ahrkyn were close friends. Brothers. But in front of strangers, only respect would be accepted.

Ahrkyn lifted a hand before Jhelan had a chance to question the wisdom of contradicting his Prince.

"I will not send your mate into danger. And she said herself she is adept with both sword and bow. Strap her to Little Dove," the Prince's lips twitched, "cover her in battle gear, and make sure she has the weapons she needs. If anything arises, we will ensure she is brought back behind the wall immediately."

Jhelan's nostrils flared as he inhaled deeply. He had been tasked with looking after Valdis, had been ordered by Ahrkyn to watch over her, to keep her safe, and help her heal. He had fought that order and lost.

Then he had begun to see Valdis for what she was, to see the strength in her heart, had laughed at her sense of humor.

Now, after only weeks, they carried matching brands of a Bond very few Elves were blessed to experience.

He had never felt so many emotions and so strongly. Not about anyone. Not about anything. The need to keep her safe surpassed everything in the world. Truth be told, he would be willing to turn his back on his Prince, on his King and Queen, on all of Ahdlai if it would keep her out of harm's way.

But it wouldn't.

If he ran with her, they would always run. They would always be at risk of the *Ihllr*, or vampires, or Shape-Shifters tracking them and taking her away from him.

If he ran with her, he might very well be considered the enemy by the people he had loved and protected since the moment he was named a member of the guard.

Jhelan turned to look at Valdis over his shoulder. She had pushed to her feet and nodded at him. He could turn his back on everyone else, but not Valdis. She looked determined. She looked angry. She looked like she was ready for a little revenge.

Of course she would want revenge. How stupid of him. Not once during all the back and forth of the men at the table, not once since she had spoken up with her own plan had he considered the option she might *want* to encounter members of the *Ihllr*. They had taken her people from her. They had taken her friends, her Clan.

She deserved vengeance. He truly hoped it wouldn't happen, truly hoped a battle didn't ensue when she was near, but he couldn't deny her this. He couldn't deny her need to avenge all that she had lost.

"Fine," he blurted.

A slow smile spread on her face. It wasn't the one he had come to adore. No; this one was full of hate, full of fire and anger. It was a smile full of unspent violence.

"Will you please sit now?" he asked.

The smile changed and she rolled her eyes. But she did, indeed, sit. Because he had agreed to this plan didn't mean he wanted her to damage her healing foot.

Jhelan continued to stand near his mate, but focused more closely on the job at hand. It was more imperative than ever that every single detail was nailed down. If he missed anything, Valdis could be put at risk.

"Are your people willing to fight alongside Ahdlai?" King Nhaeem asked the ogre.

Brizio silently consulted his companions. Jhelan didn't know whether one or all of them were telepaths or whether they had come to know each other well enough to speak with simply a glance.

Whichever it was, all three nodded in unison before Brizio turned his attention back to the King.

"We three are willing. We will have to return to the Coven to ask the others. We will not speak for them."

"Let your people know we would be grateful for any help they can spare. My only wish is to keep my people safe. I will be in your debt for any help you offer," the King said, his fist against his chest.

Jhelan wasn't one to ask favors because he didn't like to owe them. But he understood exactly why the King would allow himself to be put in such a position – if the *Ihllr* conjured enough warriors to overrun the guard of Ahdlai, the city and their way of life would fall. The King was willing to be in someone's debt to keep that from happening.

Brizio and the two witches stood, bowed deeply at the waist, then left the room.

It was now up to the guard of Ahdlai to watch over their people. It was up to them to keep those who entrusted their lives to the men who proudly wore the emblem of Ahdlai safe.

"Take your mate home. We can handle the rest without you," Ahrkyn ordered.

Jhelan frowned at him. That was the second time he had referred to Valdis as Jhelan's mate. He must have noticed their brands.

When he glanced at the rest of the men, he noticed not a single one looked in Valdis's direction. They were avoiding the risk of sending Jhelan into a possessive rage. He would have no control over his actions if it appeared another was ogling his mate.

While every halfling carried human blood in their veins, they were still part Elf. And every non-human he had ever met, save the Fae, went through a phase similar to a wild animal during rutting season. Jhelan would fight anyone and everyone who touched his mate. He would even attack if a look lingered too long.

It was primal, and, at times, annoying. But completely out of his control.

Take your mate home.

Ahrkyn knew exactly why Jhelan was so distracted. Jhelan had completed the Bond without being buried inside Valdis. He needed to ensure they were connected in every worldly way possible. Were she of Elven blood instead of Fae, he might have suggested a blood exchange ceremony. But neither was that her tradition nor known whether it would have an adverse reaction to her system.

Jhelan didn't ask whether the Prince was sure, didn't ask the King permission to be excused. Merely turned, lifted Valdis into his arms, and rushed them through the house and onto the lawn.

Little Dove was tied to a post nearby where she had been left earlier. And she would be there when he was done making love with his mate unless someone else put her in the stall or released her into the paddock.

Valdis's arms were locked around his neck, her hair blew in the wind, trailing behind her, her chest heaved with each breath. He could both smell and feel her arousal. He could feel it as strongly as he felt his own, ratcheting up his own need until he thought he would go insane if he didn't have her beneath him immediately.

Had they not lived in such a populated town, had the sun not been high, Jhelan might have lost his mind and taken her right there on the Palace lawn.

But what he had planned would take time. It would take privacy. It might very well take until the morning hours.

Lust thrummed through Valdis, sending warmth to pool low in her belly. Every part of her was on fire and hypersensitive. She could hear both her own heartbeat and Jhelan's in her ear, swore she could feel the blood pumping through his veins.

And she could absolutely feel his need to be with her. It mirrored her own.

She was Untouched by choice. She feared should she allow any man to lay with her, he might attempt to Claim her. Jhelan hadn't tried, yet the Universe had marked them both, had permanently branded them both, had demanded they become one.

There was only one thing left for them to do to fully complete the Claim; he needed to finish inside of her.

She could not carry his child, had no risk of becoming pregnant, and neither of their species were susceptible to the diseases that sometimes ran rampant through human society. They were free to enjoy each other fully without fear of consequence.

Valdis nuzzled Jhelan's neck, silently begging him to move faster. He was running at preternatural speeds, but it wasn't enough. She needed him. She needed him more than her next breath.

After what felt like an eternity, he was pushing his door open and rushing them inside. He kicked it shut behind them and immediately slanted his mouth over hers, the fierceness stealing her breath and quickening her heart rate.

Jhelan didn't stop walking, didn't stop carrying her through the house until he was to the bedroom where he gently laid her on the bed, following her down and covering her body with his own.

His lips devoured her mouth, his tongue danced and dueled with hers. His hand roamed her side, raising to clasp her breast through her tunic.

Naked. She needed to be naked. She needed him naked. She needed to feel his skin against hers, needed to feel him covering her, entering her, owning every inch of her body as she took possession of his.

"I need you," he whispered as his lips trailed to the hollow below her ear then nipped at her throat.

"I need you," she whispered back.

Jhelan pushed back until he was sitting on his haunches and began peeling away the layers of his battle leathers.

She would definitely need help with the vest he'd insisted she wear when they had taken their minor, short-lived adventure into the woods.

When his top half was bare, Valdis's mouth went dry. She had seen him shirtless only once. But at that time, she was resentful and in so much pain she hadn't taken the time to truly enjoy the physical beauty of this man. His muscles were strong and cultivated from years of fighting and hard work. The brand that had developed on both of their hands and forearms snaked up his bicep and wrapped around his shoulder, disappearing behind his back.

His eyes were bright, the blue she had come to adore shone with iridescence as his gaze roamed her from head to toe.

"I'm not sure whether I want to see you naked or continue seeing you look like a warrior," he said, his voice deep and growly.

"Naked," she demanded.

Her own voice sounded husky in her ears as her need grew. Feeling the emotions of Jhelan combined with hers was nearly overwhelming. She could feel his want, could feel his desperation to push into her, could feel the desire to complete their Bond.

A feral smile spread on his face as he lowered his hands and began to work at the latches and straps of the leather vest. She sat up so he could push the leather off her shoulders then pull her tunic over her head.

She was now fully on display. He didn't rush to remove his breeches, simply soaked her in, focusing longer on her breasts and the apex between her thighs covered by a curly thatch of hair.

"So beautiful," he whispered with so much reverence it nearly brought tears to Valdis's eyes. The glow in his eyes intensified. "Mine," he growled.

He still didn't remove his breaches. Instead, he kissed a path from her throat, stopping at her breasts to show them attention, lapping at her nipples before sucking each into his mouth, then pressed kisses to her stomach and nipped at her ribs.

She wiggled when his long hair and love bites tickled, the giggle in her throat changing to a moan when his mouth found her core. His tongue made a long, slow swipe through her folds. He then made love to her with his mouth.

Valdis had wondered how it would feel if she ever gave herself to a man, had fantasized how it would feel to have hands or a mouth on her. Nothing she had ever conjured in her imagination came close to the ecstasy she now experienced.

"Jhelan," she moaned as he took her sensitive nub between his lips and sucked.

Pressure built low in her belly, demanding release. She would lose her mind if that pressure didn't ease soon, yet she didn't want him to stop teasing her with his mouth.

As she shifted her legs on the mattress and gripped the sheets on either side of her, little explosions lit behind her closed lids. She imploded from the middle out.

Opening her mouth, she released a cry as wave after wave of pleasure rippled over her, through her, taking her under until she wondered if it would ever end.

Jhelan pushed from the end of the bed, shoved his breeches to his ankles and kicked them off. Climbing up her body, he reached between them and positioned the head of his cock against her opening.

"This might hurt a moment. If it's too much, tell me. I promise I would never hurt you."

Slowly, he pushed into her, inch by tantalizing inch. There was a pinch but no pain.

His hips moved in slow circles, working her, loosening her, until he was fully embedded inside of her warmth, his hips pressed against hers.

Jhelan's breath sawed in and out of his lungs and a muscle jumped in his cheek as he gritted his teeth with the need to move. But he was putting her needs above his own, taking it slowly to prevent causing her any discomfort.

Within moments, that pinch faded and all she could feel was Jhelan, the hard length of him pumping slowly in and out of her. He held his weight off of her on his elbows, his forearms and dark curtain of hair framing her face.

"So beautiful," he muttered again as he stared down at her.

She could tell he was still holding back, or perhaps he was savoring their first time together. She didn't care which, as long as he didn't stop moving. More pressure had begun to build. Already, another orgasm was teetering on the edge, begging her closer, waiting to take her under again, waiting to push her over the precipice.

The brands on Valdis's arm began to burn, or rather tingle, the sensation moving up her arm and over her shoulder. She hadn't bothered to check to see if they matched Jhelan's. She had been far too interested in seeing him naked than examining her arm.

But as that sensation began to heat and throb, a sense of…rightness, of peace came over her. It was as though every single moment of her life suddenly made sense, like she had truly found her home.

And that home was in Jhelan's arms, in his home, in his heart.

Jhelan continued to clench his jaw as he tried to make their first time last. He had tried to avoid her discomfort by depriving himself of release.

She might not have been Touched before this moment, but she knew enough to know how to please a man.

Shoving his chest, she pushed him off her and onto his back, then straddled his waist. She did as he had done and reached between their bodies to guide his cock to her core, then lowered, taking all of him slowly.

His eyes rolled closed and he moaned, the sound growly, deep, and felt as though it vibrated against every erogenous point on her body.

From this position, Valdis was in control. She knew he needed release. She needed another.

She had no intention of keeping their pace anything but what they both needed – frantic, desperate, hurried. Hungry.

And she was. She was hungry for him. Hungry to feel him fill her, hungry to see him fall apart, hungry to watch his face as she brought him pleasure.

"Valdis," he moaned, his eyes squeezed shut as his hips began to rise to meet hers until their pace caused the bed to shake, the headboard thumping against the wall.

She had always wondered what it would be like to finally lie with a man. She was filled with joy that she had waited for the person the Universe had created specifically for her. She was filled with joy that she had waited for Jhelan.

Those little tremors and implosions began low in her belly and radiated out, causing Valdis to throw her head back and cry out.

Jhelan followed her, his hands tightening on her hips as he barked out her name and thrust his hips upward, filling her with his seed.

It took a few moments before either of them could speak as they sucked in breath after breath, filling their lungs with much needed oxygen.

She collapsed onto his chest, turning her head to rest her cheek on his shoulder.

His hands made small, soft movements along her spine, up to her neck, then down again.

This was perfection. This moment, right here with Jhelan, was utter and complete perfection, more than she could have ever dreamed of having in her lifetime.

It wasn't a fantasy. She hadn't settled for someone who didn't deserve her trust, someone who didn't deserve to own all of her.

She had unknowingly waited for Jhelan. And he now owned her, heart, body, and soul.

Chapter Ten

Jhelan laid on his back, Valdis's head resting on his shoulder, her arm across his waist, her leg draped over his thighs, affectively pinning him to the mattress.

She had fallen asleep some time ago. But he didn't have the heart to move and rouse her. She needed rest to heal. Her heart would take far longer, but she was so close to having the binding removed from her foot. Then she would need time to rebuild the strength in her legs.

His fingers toyed with her long golden hair as her breath came in slow, steady draws. As much as he'd wanted her, he had no idea how different the world would feel after.

His brand had grown warm and throbbed as they'd made love. They had completed the Bond. They were unified until one of them died. And, being as both species were long lived, that could be centuries from now.

Please let it be centuries. He knew if she left this world before him, he would follow shortly after. Now that he'd found her, there was no way he could go a day without her at his side.

The possessive urge to keep her locked inside these four walls grew. He wanted no men to see her, wanted no men near her. But that was both unrealistic and idiotic. Not only could he not keep her from living her life, he knew damned well she would fight him tooth and nail. And she would win.

She wasn't the kind of woman to back down from a fight. He had learned that from the day he had found her.

What a fateful day. It had been ordinary, just another in the long line of patrols he had run with the guard, another battle he had fought against those who defied the region's laws.

Yet it had brought Valdis into his life.

He supposed they could be considered an odd pairing. He was at least a foot taller than her petite frame and had over a hundred pounds on her. And, while they were both halflings, she came from the same species who had tormented his people for so long.

She knew nothing of her people. As much as he would love to find some Fairies to teach her of their history, perhaps help her discover her gifts, he knew his presence would not be accepted within any Court. Silently or not, the Fae still saw all others as inferior.

As much as he loved lying here with her, both his bladder and stomach demanded action. They hadn't eaten in hours, and they had burned a lot of calories over the past few hours of exploring each other's bodies.

Slowly and carefully, he disentangled himself from her limbs, smiling when she groaned in protest.

"Where do you think you're going?" Her voice was hoarse with sleep.

"I'm starving. I'm going to make dinner. Do you want to sleep longer or would you like some food?"

Valdis rolled onto her back and looked at him through sleepy eyes. Her lips were kiss swollen, the skin around her mouth was red from the whiskers he hadn't bothered to shave in days, her hair was sprawled on the pillow below her head.

She looked like a goddess. She looked like an offering meant only for him.

"I can't tempt you back to bed?"

She lifted both knees and opened and closed them like a butterfly.

"You'll be the death of me," he said, pouncing on her, causing the bed to jostle and shake.

Valdis giggled and squealed as he dramatically kissed and nibbled across her shoulder blades.

"Why do we ever have to leave this bed?" she asked.

He settled on his stomach, propping his chin on her ribs, and looked into her face. "Were it up to me, we would stay right here and have food and supplies delivered to us. That way, I can find more ways to make you giggle."

He poked her ribs, causing her to jerk and swat at his hand.

"Will it always be like this?"

Though still smiling, he furrowed his brows, scrunching his forehead in confusion. "What do you mean?"

"Will we always feel like this?" She waved her hand between the two of them. "Two weeks ago, the mere sight of you reminded me of all I've lost. It made me angry. Now, I can't stand the thought of you walking through that door when it's time for you to return to your duties."

His heart began to race. "Does that mean you'll stay when you're healed?"

Her cheeks deepened to a pretty shade of pink. "Do you want me to stay?"

Jhelan reached across her body to grab the wrist of her left arm and held it against his own. "These are like chains. They have bound me to you in a way nothing else ever could. I go where you go. If you choose to leave, I will be at your side. But if you choose to stay, I will spend every minute of every day making you thankful for that choice."

"You know I can't give you an heir."

"I know."

"And you should know I will not share you. I won't allow you to Claim another female to breed."

He sighed as though put out. "Fine. I guess I'll save all my attention for you."

She rolled her eyes but couldn't hide her smile.

"This Bond would not allow me to lay with another woman. It would cause me as much pain as it would you. I don't want anyone else. I trust Mother Universe. I trust that she's brought us together to form the perfect union."

She turned her hand so she could thread her fingers through his.

"This brand, this mark, it links us both emotionally and physically. I assume you've felt me?"

Her smile turned wry. "In more ways than one."

He began to harden at her words, but he needed her to know all of it before he took her again. And he had every intention of doing exactly that. At least twice more before they slept through the night.

"I can feel your emotions as you feel mine. I would also be able to find you should you become lost...or taken. As you would be able to find me."

Her eyes narrowed. "So, if you were to wander away and find yourself a pretty lady, I could track you down and beat the hell out of you?"

He chuckled, his chin tickling her ribs enough for her to jerk away a bit.

"Yes. You could. But I swear on my own soul, you will never have to worry about my eyes straying. My heart is yours, Valdis. From now until eternity."

She pressed her free hand to his cheek as a sensation began to tickle his senses.

Something was off. Something wasn't right.

It wasn't Valdis. All he felt from her was affection. Contentment. Happiness.

It was in the air. Tension built until it was nearly suffocating.

And then the scent hit his nose.

Lunging from the bed, he hastily donned his battle gear. "Get dressed. Stay in this room. Do not leave for any reason."

Her brows dropped as her eyes widened.

"What is it?"

"Someone is here. They have not been invited nor are they welcome."

Shouts emphasized his words as the guards on duty around the wall called for backup.

Had the *Ihllr* come early? Had they attacked before the Palace was ready or before they could discover whether the witches would lend them aid?

"I need a weapon," she said after him as he rushed through the door.

"You are not going out there."

A thump sounded on the floor in the bedroom. She was on her feet and moving toward him, the hops and hobbles accented by grunts.

He turned to find her standing in the doorway. "I won't go with you. But I won't stay here unarmed. I refuse to go down without a fight if someone gets past the guard."

Jhelan knew her words to be truth. He had seen the damage done to her when she'd fought the last time. Had seen the fire in her eyes as she'd grabbed the only thing she could find littering the forest floor and swung it at him in a last ditch effort to protect herself and prevent being taken by monsters.

Hurrying from the room, he grabbed a sword and a few daggers, handing them to her when he was near enough.

"Please. I'm begging you to stay in this house. We are trained for this. You'll be a target."

"I'll be a distraction," she said, understanding the words he didn't say. "I'll stay here," she promised.

She gripped the lapel of his vest and pulled him close, rising onto her toes to press a desperate, hasty kiss to his lips. "Please come back to me."

He kissed her back. "Always."

Jhelan then did the hardest thing he had ever done in his life – he turned his back on his brand-new mate and left her alone while he went to seek and destroy the enemy.

Valdis pulled a tunic over her head, then struggled to strap the vest back on that Jhelan had removed when they'd first entered the room. The leather might not keep someone from carrying her away, but it would at least protect her torso from any blades aimed for her heart.

She had finally succumbed to the Universe's push, had allowed a man into her heart, had allowed herself to grow attached to him, and now, she would once again wait to learn her future's fate.

She had survived alone for years. Even when with her Clan, she had always kept her heart guarded, always kept a wall around her emotions. It was the only thing that was keeping her from falling apart at the loss of so many.

But that had never stopped her from doing what she could to protect them.

Now, she could only focus on protecting herself. She wasn't able to run into the town to keep others safe. She would have to depend on Jhelan and the guard to do that. She would have to trust they wouldn't let any trespassers through the wall.

What if they had brought the vampires and others as the ogre had warned? What if the guard was overrun? Then what? Valdis could fight, but she currently only had one good foot.

Didn't matter. She would swing the sword with all her might at anyone who attempted to come near. She would either throw the daggers or use them for hand-to-hand combat. And she would pray she could hold off the enemy until Jhelan got to her.

He had to get to her. She no longer feared so much for her own life as much as she did his. He had just run headfirst into unknown danger.

Her brand began to throb. Focusing on the Bond between them, she swore she could practically see the world through his eyes as she tapped into his emotions.

Anger. Curiosity. Rage. Fear. So many feelings flooded his veins and rushed straight to her heart.

Fear. For himself? Or for the town?

She knew he would worry for Valdis's safety, which, of course, was the only reason she had promised to stay within the bedroom and behind locked doors. She would be exactly what she'd said – a distraction. And that kind of distraction could get Jhelan or one of the others killed.

She could hear no signs of battle, but there were constant shouts, orders being given, residents warned to stay within their homes.

As if any walls or windows could keep out the Shape-Shifters or vampires had they arrived with the *Ihllr* Elves.

Breathe, Valdis. Just breathe.

She didn't want her anxiety to feed through their Bond and cause Jhelan any panic. She was safe. She was fine. It was him she was anxious over, his safety for which she feared.

Instead of focusing on her own emotions, she closed her eyes and ran along the wall with Jhelan in her mind. She focused on the beat of his heart, on the cadence of his feet as they hit the lawn, on the determination flooding his system with adrenaline as he sought the interloper.

Seconds turned to minutes. Those minutes dragged on. And still she followed Jhelan through their Bond, knew where he was at any moment, knew exactly how he felt, knew the exact moment the danger was over.

She sighed with relief as his heartrate slowed and felt his need to return to her side. But as the head of the Royal guard, he had a job to do first. She would wait patiently. She would be there with open arms. She would cover him with her scent, take him into her in every way possible, then finally they could fall asleep in each other's arms.

A knock on the front door startled her.

Valdis searched for Jhelan through their link. It wasn't him, but he wasn't far. He would know if the enemy was literally at the front door.

Carefully, she made her way from the bedroom and peeked around the corner through the glass of the door.

Ihsander.

"Is it locked?" she called out.

He tried the knob then nodded.

Well, shit.

Hobbling her way through the house, she was panting by the time she made it to the door and let Jhelan's friend inside.

"Jhelan wanted me to check on you and let you know everything is safe. He asked me to stay with you until he returns."

"Why would he ask you to stay if everything is safe?"

Ihsander's shoulders rose and fell. "It's a Bonded male thing. He'll forever be extremely protective of you. But I'll ask that you stay well away from me until he returns. If I'm too close, he'll accuse me of…well, *whatever* and attack me whether provoked or deserved."

"He'll have to get over that real quick," she muttered.

Grabbing the chair pushed under the dining table, she pulled it free and dropped on to it heavily.

It was getting easier to put weight on her broken foot, but only for short periods of time. Each step still sent ripples of pain through her nerve endings. But the healer had assured her it would only be another week or two before the bindings could be removed and she could retrain her foot and strengthen her leg.

"Are you hungry?" Ihsander asked as he made his way into the kitchen.

He didn't bother asking where anything was as he opened and closed cabinets, pulling out various ingredients.

"I assume you are," she teased.

These guys were always hungry. If they weren't ready to sit down for a meal, they had something in their satchels to snack on.

"Jhelan was getting ready to make dinner when…whoever showed up."

"We think they were testing our security. Trying to find a weakness."

"Did they? Find a weakness, I mean?"

He shrugged as he threw together a few pieces of meat on some fresh baked bread for simple sandwiches. No vegetables. No seasoning. Just meat and bread.

After setting one on a plate and pouring Valdis a glass of tea, he set her serving on the table, then seated himself across the room on the couch.

"You're not joking about staying away from me," she said, turning in her chair to watch him.

His first bite took up nearly a quarter of his sandwich. Mouth full and cheeks puffed, he shook his head. It took a few moments for him to chew and swallow before he spoke again.

"It's the Bond. He has no control over it. Don't hold it against him."

Holding her arm up, she waved it slowly at Ihsander. "Can you see them? The brands?"

"Yeah, but they're faint. They almost look like scars to the rest of the world. I hear they're dark to you guys, though."

"Yeah. They look like…kind of like the tattoos humans used to cover their skin with in the old days."

He grunted and took another bite.

"So, what happened?" she asked, then started on her own sandwich.

Jhelan would have prepared a lot more. But this was fine for now and would hold her over. She figured he would be famished by the time he returned from his duties.

"About a dozen Shape-Shifters attempted to infiltrate the wall. A few caused a distraction at the gate while others were circled around the entire perimeter. They were trying to find a way in without being detected."

"Where are they now?" she asked with her mouth full.

He wrinkled his nose. "I get that you were raised in the woods, but were you never taught not to speak with your mouth full."

She rolled her eyes and waved for him to answer her question.

"Those who weren't killed have been taken before the King for questioning."

"What will happen after they're questioned?"

Ihsander dropped back against the couch cushion. "If they are forthcoming with useful information, they might be spared, kept in the cellar. If not…"

"Executed?" she asked.

He pointed a finger at her as he nodded, then popped the last bite of his sandwich into his mouth.

She tried but couldn't find any pity for those who had attempted to infiltrate the area. They would have passed the houses to get to the walls. That part creeped her a little. Why hadn't the Royal Family built a wall around the entirety of the town to keep all its inhabitants safe?

Had they walked past Jhelan's house while he and Valdis had made love? While she'd slept? Had they looked into windows of the residents of Ahdlai?

Valdis shivered at the thought. At least in the forest, they would have heard steps crunching on dead leaves or twigs. Being a paranormal being herself, she would have caught the scent wafting on the air of any encroaching on their home.

How had the Shape-Shifters passed so many people without being detected? They could shift into the form of whatever animal that slept inside their bodies, but they couldn't exactly become invisible.

Valdis finished her sandwich, then looked to Ihsander.

"What do you want to do while we wait for my mate to return?"

"I plan on staying right here until then. Unless you need help going to bed. I was given permission to carry you wherever needed. Any more than that, I'm afraid he'll think my scent on you means something completely different."

Her life had changed so much in such a short amount of time. Jhelan and Valdis didn't know each other as well as they would one day, but he would have to learn to get used to the presence of other men near her.

Especially since she had every intention of requesting further training from the guard the moment she was fully healed.

Chapter Eleven

Jhelan, Ahdeben, Ahrkyn, and several other guard members stood in a semicircle around the four Shape-Shifters forced to their knees before the King by the guard who had captured them.

"As I see it, there are two choices: You tell us everything you know, or you will be taken outside and put down. Do you need a moment to decide?" King Nhaeem said.

The King of Ahdlai was fair. He was kind. He opened his doors to those who needed help, welcomed the mothers of Elven offspring to live within the town.

But he would not allow anyone to risk the lives and safety of his family or people.

"Fuck off," one of the Shape-Shifters said.

King Nhaeem raised his eyes to Ahdeben. It appeared this male would become an example for the others.

Ahdeben moved forward, called forth his magic, and practically fried the man's brains while still inside his skull. Blood and other fluids poured from his eyes, nose, mouth, and ears.

His buddies gaped and began to try to move away from the goo that formed a growing puddle on the marble floor.

The dead man swayed, then fell face first, dead before he hit the ground.

"Anyone else?" King Nhaeem asked.

Had the situation not been so dire, Jhelan might have barked out a laugh. The King looked so casual, as though he were asking if anyone was interested in another serving of cake rather than the opportunity to avoid having their brains scrambled.

"This was not our doing," one male said.

He refused to raise his eyes to the King, refused to acknowledge those around him. He had been the first to throw up his hands when the Shape-Shifters had been caught. He'd put up no fight at all.

"Yet you were the ones we found," Prince Ahrkyn said.

He stood nearest his father, his hands clasped before him as he glared down at the captives. There were only four of them. Well, three now. The rest had been killed when they'd attempted to fight the guard.

"You think we have a choice? We're no better than the humans out in the woods. We struggle to survive, yet your kind treats us like dogs. Worse than dogs. At least those, you keep as pets. You treat kindly. You feed them and give them shelter."

"If you want to be treated better, why the hell do you continuously band with the wrong side?" Ahdeben asked.

Another man snorted. "We band with whoever offers us enough food."

His statement caught Jhelan off guard. These men were willing to put their lives on the line for food. That was it. Food. They weren't being paid in gold or cash as the humans used in earlier times. There was no use for either of those things in the modern world. Food and fresh water were of the highest currency.

The humans foraged and hunted to the best of their abilities. The Shape-Shifters could shift into animal form to take down larger prey. But they were unable to stay in one place long enough for anything more than that.

"Take them to the cells. I must think," King Nhaeem ordered.

Ahdeben, Jhelan, Ahrkyn, and the other guards hoisted the men to their feet and began to usher them out.

"Ahrkyn and Jhelan, please remain behind. We must speak."

Jhelan exchanged a look with Ahrkyn, but stepped out of formation to join the King as he rose from his throne and sauntered into the dining room.

King Nhaeem removed his crown and set it on the table. He dropped heavily onto the chair at the head of the table.

"How close did they get?" he asked.

Ahrkyn sat to his father's right, Jhelan sat on the King's left.

"They were able to sneak past the houses in town without detection," Jhelan admitted.

It wasn't until his senses had alerted him to approaching danger and he felt the tension from the guards at the gate that he had known something was amiss.

"Are they able to mask their scent? How did no one smell their arrival?"

Jhelan looked to Ahrkyn, hoping his Prince and friend would have an answer. When Ahrkyn's shoulders rose and fell, that hope was dashed.

"I've rarely encountered Shape-Shifters. I have no idea what they're capable of. I always assumed they were nothing more than thieves and beggars. They always tend to be with whatever party is raiding a town," Jhelan said.

"Do you believe the words of the one who spoke?" the King asked Jhelan.

Had he been asked that question a month ago, he would have called the man a liar. He would have accused him of attempting to appeal to the *Vhtir's* sense of pity and compassion.

But after learning about the way Valdis had lived her whole life, after learning how the humans who preferred to live on the outskirts of society lived, his opinion had changed.

"I do."

"You believe they simply latch on to whoever promises them a full belly?" King Nhaeem asked.

"I was a child when the humans went to war. I was barely ten when non-humans took control of the planet. But I remember how it was before, how we had to remain in the shadows, how those like Elves with our pointy ears were unable to blend into human society. I remember going to bed hungry. And there was far more prey to be hunted in those years. If these people, these Shape-Shifters truly are struggling to feed their families, why wouldn't they do what was needed?"

"The humans don't align themselves with the *Ihllr*," Ahrkyn pointed out.

Jhelan huffed out a laugh lacking humor. "Because they would become victims. The *Ihllr* can't breed with the Shape-Shifter women. The price would be far too high for any human Clan to join a group like the *Ihllr* or vampires."

The King rubbed both hands down his face as though weariness weighed heavily on him.

Jhelan knew the feeling. He wasn't so much physically tired as mentally and emotionally. The fear he'd felt that his home, his town, and his mate were under attack had caused his heart to race and ice to chill his veins.

He had done his best to filter through the barrage of emotions as he'd detected the concern Valdis felt for him and focused on ensuring there were no others hiding in wait for an attack.

"Feed the prisoners. Ensure they're comfortable. But do no release them. Perhaps in time, the others will talk. Keep them separate so they cannot form a plan of escape or develop a lie," the King said.

"I'll have additional guards positioned around the town instead of simply the wall. We have become complacent in our security. Those men were able to saunter past six homes containing guards as well trained as myself. It won't happen again," Jhelan vowed, placing his fist to his heart and bowing his head.

"I trust you, Jhelan. Next to my son, you have been the only guard in my employ who has never let me down."

The King stood and exited with no parting words, leaving Ahrkyn and Jhelan alone at the table.

"You completed the Bond," Ahrkyn said, his eyes dipping to the brands on Jhelan's arms.

They should have been slightly darker to others now that he had buried himself in Valdis's body, yet still faint and silvery.

"We have."

"Were you…"

"Were we making love when the Shape-Shifters approached? No. I was preparing to make dinner for myself and my mate. I sensed something was off."

"Your precognition has grown over the years. Pity it isn't strong enough to give us more time to prepare for any further attacks."

His precognition was nothing more than a feeling he got deep in his gut, something that made the magic in his blood awaken to alert him of possible danger. That only helped when the danger was nearby. It didn't warn him of anything in the future.

"I'm surprised you sent Ihsander," Ahrkyn said.

The Prince's lips twitched at the corner.

"Ihsander seeks to sire an heir. She is of no use to him. And he has my trust."

"You mean he knows full well you'll rip his cock from his body if you suspect him of touching your mate."

Jhelan chuckled. "Something like that."

"It'll fade."

"What will?"

"The possessive urge to rip to shreds any man who looks in your mate's direction."

"How would you know?" Jhelan asked.

The King had been on Ahrkyn for years to sire an heir, to carry on the bloodline of the Royal Family.

But Ahrkyn had no desire to be a father. He had no desire to Claim a female. He was content sating his needs as the rest of them did – with any willing female Elf. There was no possibility of producing offspring in that matter. And the odds of developing a Bond such as Valdis and Jhelan's was rare.

Ahrkyn made a dismissive sound in the back of his throat and gave Jhelan an obscene gesture with his hand.

"Return to your mate. I'll deal with the guard," Ahrkyn said.

As much as Jhelan wanted mothing more, he could not. There was much to be done before he could fall into Valdis's arms for the night.

"I have work to do first. Ihsander will watch over her."

"Is that enough to keep your urges under control?"

Jhelan chuckled deep and low. "Depends. Of which urge do you speak?"

Ihsander did exactly as he had said and stayed no closer than ten feet to Valdis at all times. He had helped her hobble to the couch so she could raise her foot onto a cushion, but then returned to the seat she'd vacated at the table.

"I really don't think he'll go crazy if you sit on the couch with me."

Ihsander snorted. "You'll see."

"Oh, no I won't. Because I won't put up with nonsense like that. You and I were friends before this happened," she said, raising her arms to reveal the brands, "and that won't change now."

Ihsander placed a hand over his heart and batted his lashes at her. "Aw. You said we're friends."

Valdis sighed and dropped her head back against the arm of the couch. "I changed my mind."

Ihsander sat up straight around the same time Valdis's brands began to tingle. Jhelan was nearby. He was returning to her as he had promised.

Two hours had passed since he'd rushed through the front door, but she had been able to track his emotions and his location the entire time. Perhaps the Bond wasn't such a bad thing. If anything else went awry, she would know his every step, she would know if he was injured, she would know when he would be in her arms again.

His heavy boots thumped up the stairs and across the small deck. Then his face was visible through the glass of the door as she practically hung off the back of the couch in anticipation.

"What happened?" she asked the moment he opened the door.

Rather than answer, he crossed the room, took her face in both hands, and pressed his lips to hers in a searing kiss.

She was practically breathless when he pulled away.

"All good?" Ihsander asked.

"One down. The rest are in cells. King Nhaeem wants to keep them separate so they can't come up with a convincing lie or try to devise a plan of escape."

"Did you learn anything from those you captured?" Valdis asked.

He rounded the couch and dropped onto the cushion beside her like his body weighed more than his legs could handle.

"Only one spoke. He said they joined the *Ihllr* because they were promised supplies."

"What kind of supplies?" Ihsander asked.

"Food."

Valdis nodded. As much as she hated the *Ihllr* and hated that the Shape-Shifters had interrupted a beautiful night, she could understand why they would agree to help. It was hard to live in the forest, hard to find enough food to feed one person, let alone a group. It was even harder if that group had children.

"You think it was justified?" Jhelan asked her.

She bobbed her head side to side. "In a way. Hunger will make you do things you never thought yourself capable. Especially if you're feeding others. You might be able to sacrifice yourself, but few would watch someone they care for suffer and starve to death."

"They attacked the city," Ihsander said, anger evident all over his face and in his voice.

"Not technically," Jhelan said.

"Close enough."

"What happened? What did they do?" Valdis asked.

"They were trying to find our weak points. Then they would report back. They were trying to figure out how they could get the *Ihllr* and whoever else they teamed up with through our walls."

"What's the point? Doesn't the *Ihllr* have their own region? Their own King or ruler or whatever?" Valdis asked.

"Why did rulers throughout the history of the world constantly battle with others? To gain more power, more land, more wealth," Jhelan said.

Valdis grunted. "The only wealth left in this world is food...wait, could they be struggling?"

"Who?"

"The *Ihllr*. They're constantly out hunting down females to breed. Could they be struggling to feed their own people?"

Jhelan scratched the stubble peppering his cheeks and jaw. He'd been cleanly shaven when she had met him. She really liked the rugged look on him.

"At this point, there's no way to know exactly what their motivation is. They have always and will always be unstable. That was why the *Vhtir* forced them out of our region and away from our people."

"Lot of good that did," Ihsander mumbled.

"Did the prisoners say how many others there are? How many are coming? When they plan to come?" Valdis asked.

Jhelan cocked a brow at her. "You think like a guardsman."

"I was a guard for my people, along with others. I'm used to protecting others. I'm used to always looking for a solution to any and every problem presented."

A smile full of affection and respect tugged up his kissable lips.

"They didn't say anything more than what I've told you both. We're hoping to learn more over the next few days."

"If we have a few days," Ihsander muttered. "You need me anymore? I'm hungry and need a shower."

"You didn't feed my mate?"

Ihsander held up his hands. "I made her a sandwich."

Jhelan looked to Valdis. She smiled and shrugged. It had held her over. Now she felt bad that Jhelan would think he would need to cook her a full meal before they went to bed for the night. But she knew he was famished. He hadn't had a chance to eat dinner before rushing out to investigate.

Ihsander left through the front door, waving over his shoulder before closing the door behind him.

"You did well," Valdis said.

"With what?"

"I could feel that. I could feel the jealousy, the possessive urge when Ihsander was here. And you didn't act on it. Thank you."

"I knew the feeling was irrational. He was nowhere near you when I stepped onto the porch."

"And had he been sitting directly beside me, you still wouldn't have had a good reason to act on those feelings."

She turned so she could cup his cheeks, the whiskers prickling her palms, and looked into his eyes.

"I want no one but you, Jhelan. I have never wanted a man the way I want you. I have never once in my life considered living anywhere but in the wild, but I have changed everything I am...for you."

"I don't want you to change for me," he said, his voice so soft.

"I just want to be near you. Your job is here. Your people are here. So, I'll stay."

His cheeks swelled against her palms as he grinned. "They're your people now. Remember that. Any single person in this town or behind the wall would protect you as much as you would protect them."

Images of the Flora and the other small children she had seen walking through the gardens or playing within town sent anxiety burning through her system. It wasn't safe for them outside the walls. At least not until they knew exactly what kind of risk they were facing.

"You should speak to King Nhaeem about allowing the families with small children to stay within the walls. For now, anyway."

"I already planned to. The fact so many Shape-Shifters were able to sneak past the homes of guards scares me. What if it had been a full attack? By the time we were aware, it might have been too late to protect the people. All we could have done was fight for our own lives and do our best to protect the Royal Family."

"And all those people would have been slaughtered. Or taken."

Jhelan wrapped an arm around Valdis's shoulders and hugged her tightly.

"I could feel you the whole time," Valdis said.

"I could feel you, too. You were unbelievably calm."

She shrugged as much as she could under his hold.

"I knew you were safe. And I figured if I felt you, you felt me. I didn't want to be a distraction and have you thinking any fear I felt was due to an attack."

"Thank you for staying inside," he said, turning his head to kiss her on top of the head.

"What the hell else could I have done? Ask them to sit still while I hopped over to fight them?"

He chuckled, the sound deep and rumbly in his chest.

"You have to be starving. Go fill your belly so we can go to bed…and you can fill me."

Chapter Twelve

"You need to take it easy," Jhelan called across the clearing.

He watched his mate training with younger members of the guard and fought tooth and nail not to rip their heads off when she was unable to block a hit.

"Don't scare them off," Valdis called back.

She had made a compelling argument as she'd healed. She was already good with weapons; there was no reason she couldn't be a secret weapon should anyone make it through the town without detection again.

He didn't like it, but he had learned his mate was headstrong and used to being independent. She'd survived her whole life without him. He had to trust she was making the best decision for her own safety.

Although, Jhelan wondered whether the extra training was because she wanted to help keep the town safe, not herself.

The younger guards, those who were not yet allowed in the field with Jhelan and the others, watched him warily each time they sparred with Valdis. They had tried to keep their distance, but she would attack them in earnest and force them to defend themselves or end up injured.

Valdis's foot had fully healed weeks ago and the healer gave her the go-ahead to begin using it, slowly at first.

It didn't matter what the healer ordered. Valdis had pushed and pushed, strengthening her leg and foot far faster than any human could do.

But she wasn't human. She was a halfling and healed at an accelerated rate, just like the rest of the non-humans.

Jhelan leaned against the wall, his arms crossed over his chest, and watched his mate closely.

She was magnificent to watch. She swung her sword with such flourish, rarely missing her mark. But it was good she was being formally trained. Her skills were honed from necessity. What she would learn from the Ahdlai guard would aid her in any kind of attack, whether against one or several opponents.

She was also being taught to be on the offensive more than focusing solely on defense. She was learning to strike first and strike fast.

And it scared the hell out of him.

He loved that his mate was learning to be stronger, faster, trained like a member of the Royal guard. But he hated that she had to be put in this situation. He hated that this was the world in which they lived.

He couldn't blame himself for bringing her into their troubles; living in the forest among the humans had been far more dangerous than anything that could be thrown in Ahdlai's direction.

Ahdeben stepped in and threw his hands up. "Take a break. Get some water."

"I'm not tired," Valdis whined.

"And you're not the only one training," Ahdeben shot back.

He winked at Valdis, indicating he was only teasing, and every muscle in Jhelan's body tensed with the need to pummel his friend.

Valdis's head turned in his direction and she cocked one brow. He merely shrugged. He couldn't control how he felt, only how he behaved.

She closed the space between them and bumped him with her shoulder before leaning against the wall and sliding until she sat on her butt.

Sweat created a sheen across her face and the parts of her chest and arms that were exposed. She had been working hard for the past couple weeks and had been eating nearly as much as Jhelan and the rest of the guard.

Since she had been eating and working so hard, her body had filled out more and her muscle had become defined. She looked like a warrior instead of the broken woman he'd found in the woods.

"Any pointers?" she said between deep breaths.

"You're a natural. But you need to keep the shield up higher. Make sure you can move it when needed to block your vital points."

"It was so heavy at first. It's getting easier."

"Because you're getting stronger."

He lowered to the ground beside her and stretched his legs in front of him. It felt weird to watch the younger generation being trained rather than being one of the trainers. But he'd learned the first day Valdis had begun that he would end up hurting someone if he were one of the teachers.

Memories of the poor kid Jhelan had knocked on his ass after he had struck a blow against Valdis made him wince.

They didn't use sharp swords and the points were dulled. The worst that could have happened was a bruise.

Not true. Any one of them could endure a broken bone when training, and had in the past. Jhelan had broken quite a few during his years as a trainee.

Valdis turned her head and looked at him sideways.

"What?" he asked without looking at her.

"You're doing better than I thought you would."

He frowned down at her.

"After that first day, I thought you would try to attack anyone who sparred with me."

He huffed a laugh and leaned his head against the wall. "Trust me when I say it's a struggle."

"Like I said, you're doing better than I thought you would. Just remember – your mom was a member of the guard. I know I'm not a large woman, but I was fighting off the enemy before I met any of you or received any of this training. Now, I'll be an even better fighter."

"You won't be –"

"I'm not saying I want to be in the guard," Valdis said, cutting him off before he could argue. "But it would be nice to have some form of a job. Eventually, you'll have to return to your perimeter checks and I'll be left here with nothing to do but twiddle my thumbs."

A grin stretched on his face as his body shook with a chuckle. "I'm sure the Queen will find something that'll fit your skills. Maybe you can help guard inside the walls."

Valdis stared at him long enough that he turned his head to smile at her wide eyes and her brows almost to her hairline.

"Seriously?"

He shrugged. "Why not?"

It was far safer for her within the walls. And she really was a strong fighter. Another person to help keep the Royal Family safe wasn't a bad thing. She could help with the watch towers or patrolling the walls to keep an eye out for any weak spots or entry points for the enemy.

She leaned to the side. He turned his head so she could press her lips to his. The kiss lingered only long enough for his body to harden before she pulled away.

He could feel her gratitude and excitement skitter through their Bond brands. He'd made her happy. Good. That was all he wanted, for his mate to be happy and safe.

"We're breaking for lunch," Ahdeben called from a distance away. "Your mate has worn out my students."

Valdis laughed and shook her head. "Wimps."

Jhelan pushed to his feet and offered a hand. When she slid hers into his, he pulled her to her feet and pushed hair from her face that had come loose from the braids Elabeth had helped pin to her head.

Since she'd had nothing when they found her, she had only been able to wear the clothing loaned or given to her by women of Ahdlai. She now wore her hair the way the women in town did, as well. More and more, she looked like she belonged here, like she had been here from day one rather than struggled to learn their ways.

He assumed part of it was because she wasn't born in the forest. She had a home once, a family. She'd grown up with the luxuries most non-humans enjoyed, so it wasn't such a stretch for her to grow accustomed to the scented soaps, the varied foods transported in after trades, or the adornments so many women wore in their hair or on their bodies.

"Can I ask you something?" she asked as they walked hand in hand toward the Palace.

"You can ask me anything."

"You've never told me what your gift is. I told you that I lack any magic, but I've never seen you use yours."

His smile grew sheepish. "I have extremely minor precognition. I know when something is coming, can sense the change in the air before anything major happens."

"Did you sense me? I mean, when you guys were battling the *Ihllr*, did you sense me?"

He frowned at her. He hadn't. He hadn't sensed her presence, had only heard her pained cries. And he hadn't sensed a change in his world as he usually would when something as major as Mother Universe sending him his Bonded mate would occur.

"I didn't."

"Hm."

The sound was noncommittal.

"What does that sound mean?"

Her shoulders rose and fell. "I don't know. It just seems like you would have a stronger gift. You told me about Ahdeben. Ihsander refuses to tell me his like he thinks I'll tease him about it, but I assume it's something strong. I would think if precognition was your gift, it would have told you I would be barging into your life."

He pulled his hand from hers and wrapped an arm around her shoulders, then pressed a kiss to the top of her head.

"Perhaps my gift only warns me of negative things. Because you barging into my life turned out to be the best thing that has happened in my entire existence."

She turned a smile up to him and wrapped her arm around his waist, tucking herself tightly into his side.

"Can I tell you something?"

He felt a surge of emotion as she spoke.

Pulling her to a stop, he turned her so he could look directly in her eyes.

"I told you – you can ask me or tell me anything."

"I love you. I love you more than simply being Bonded, more than being Claimed. I love you, Jhelan."

Warmth unfurled in his chest, and he sighed. Cupping her face, he tilted her head back so he could taste her lips. He deepened the kiss only enough to convey everything rushing through his heart and mind.

When he pulled back, his gaze bounced between her eyes. "I think I've loved you since the moment I saw you pick up that branch and try to bash it over my head."

She rolled her eyes, but tilted her head back in invitation. Jhelan didn't hesitate. He lowered his head and pressed another kiss to her lips, then guided her into the house, their arms still wrapped around each other.

This was what he loved best, having her in his arms and as close as they could possibly get. If he had his way, they would spend every minute of every day in bed, snuggled under the blankets or making love.

He had also learned in their time together she wasn't the kind of woman who enjoyed lounging. She had nearly gone mad waiting for her foot to heal so she no longer had to depend on someone carrying her or being trotted around on Little Dove's back.

She still rode the pony, but it was purely for enjoyment. It was obvious she'd grown fond of the mare.

Jhelan tried to picture her on the small, white pony riding beside the guard on their large horses and bit back a laugh. She was nearly half the size of the guard, and the pony was only about three quarters the size of the beasts the guard rode. Valdis would look like a child following behind.

Noise rose up the moment Jhelan pushed open the front door for his mate to walk ahead of him. The trainees would be eating in the servant's area, but the Royal guard, at least those not currently on duty, would be seated around the table as they waited for the staff to deliver the afternoon meal.

King Nhaeem was at the head at table, Queen Ahlmeda on his right, Prince Ahrkyn on his left. The rest of the table was surrounded by a sea of black leather.

Valdis had yet to be fitted with any battle gear, although she had requested some several times. So, she'd been training in a tunic and stood out nearly as much as the Queen with her ethereal beauty and vibrantly colored gown.

A loud grumble sounded from Valdis's stomach as Jhelan pulled out a chair and waited for her to sit.

He and those around her chuckled.

"Your little warrior mate needs to be fed. Have you been depriving her?" Ihsander teased.

"My little warrior mate could probably kick your ass at this point. She's been working her butt off."

"I saw. Won't be long before she'll need to move on to more advanced training."

Valdis turned her head to look up at Jhelan. "Ohhh. There's more to learn?"

"You're going to be the death of me," Jhelan said before pressing a kiss to her lips and turning to the trays that were delivered to the table.

Now that Valdis had a full belly, her body began to feel every minute she'd spent training today. She had worked every second she could to be as well trained as Jhelan and the others. Or at least as well trained as the younger guards.

Since Jhelan had been a member of the Royal guard since childhood and was the head of the organization, she doubted she would ever best him in a fight.

Her eyelids were heavy, but it was only the middle of the day. And there was still far too much training to be done, especially with a threat looming.

They had heard nothing more from Brizio the ogre or his companions in weeks. She hoped they hadn't been killed returning home. She hoped even more that their Coven hadn't outright refused to help Ahdlai if the *Ihllr* had, indeed, recruited people from other groups.

"You should release the Shape-Shifters," Valdis blurted out.

Conversation ceased so quickly it was almost comical as every head turned her way. Most of the faces staring at her wore varying expressions of curiosity while others looked at her as though she had gone mad.

"What are you saying?" King Nhaeem asked.

"You should release the Shape-Shifters. I assume they've been treated well since they've been in your custody?"

"Of course," the King said, his tone indicating she'd insulted him. "All those who enter Ahdlai's territory are treated well unless they mean my people harm."

"Release them. Or at least one of them. Let them return to their people, tell their Pack about us. Let them explain to their people how they were treated and how we are not the enemy."

"How would that help? Many of those who arrived were killed," Prince Ahrkyn said.

She inhaled a deep breath and wondered whether the next sentence was wise. "If you were to offer to feed those who are suffering, wouldn't they be willing to side with you, instead?" She turned to Jhelan. "You said the man who spoke that first night said they agreed to fight beside the *Ihllr* because they offered them supplies, food. What if we were to offer them the same thing? The prisoners could return to their people, report the conditions in which they were held, and take a message back to their own leader. They would see they're fighting on the wrong side."

"Assuming that man spoke the truth," Prince Ahrkyn said. "None have said a word since. They have refused to speak with any of our guard, my father, myself. No one. They refuse to open up about where their Pack is located."

"Of course they won't tell you that. Had you found me in any other condition, I wouldn't have told you, either. And I never saw any of you as the enemy. But we protect our own, just like you."

A muscle ticked in the King's jaw, and she wondered if she had overstepped the boundaries. She was nothing, merely mated to the head of the Royal guard. A resident of Ahdlai. And she had, more or less, challenged him and his position on the matter.

It was a few moments before King Nhaeem spoke again. The entire table remained silent. The tension in the room was palpable.

"You might have a point," he said.

It was as if the entire room released a sigh of relief at his words.

"I cannot release them all. They did, after all, attempt to infiltrate the walls of my Palace."

"Let me talk to them. I'll tell them about my experience with the *Ihllr*, about how you all found me and took me in."

"Absolutely not," Jhelan said the same time the brands leading from her fingertips to her shoulder throbbed with fear. For her.

"What could possibly happen, Jhelan? They're behind bars, right? And I'm sure you won't let me go down there alone. With any single member of the guard nearby, there's no way they could hurt me. Not to mention, I can now fight almost as well as all of you," she said, her eyes sweeping over the group listening closely.

"She has a point," Ahrkyn said.

Jhelan shot a glare in the Prince's direction. "You would allow your mate to interact with a prisoner who worked with the enemy?"

"Ah. And you see, that's one of the biggest reasons I have no desire to Claim a female. I don't have to make those kinds of decisions." He held up a hand when Jhelan opened his mouth to argue further. "She will be in no danger. You know none of us would allow that. And I've watched her in training. I think she might be able to best any single one of the prisoners in the cells." His lips twitched with a smile he held back.

"Take her to speak with him, with the male who told us their reasoning. Ihsander, go with her. Listen closely. Use your gift," King Nhaeem ordered.

Valdis tilted her head and studied Ihsander. What was his gift? She sure as hell hoped it wasn't telepathy or he would have heard more sexual fantasies about Jhelan than any man wanted to hear about his friend.

"I'm going with her," Jhelan said.

"No. You're not. Your Bond is too new, and your behavior could affect everything. I will send my son and Ahdeben with her."

"Two unmated males."

"You are the only Bond mated male in Ahdlai besides myself. You need to trust my judgement and remember your place," the King said.

Valdis could feel frustration pulsing through her as if it were her own. But Jhelan bowed his head and placed a fist to his chest.

"You may proceed when you choose, Valdis," the King said.

She looked around the table and nodded. She would wait for her chaperones to finish their meal. Then she would see what she could learn about the Shape-Shifters and try to win them over to her side. To *their* side.

To the right side.

Chapter Thirteen

Valdis struggled to keep her nerves steady. Jhelan would feel everything she did. She didn't want him to defy the King and rush downstairs thinking she was in danger.

She had never visited a jail cell during her travels, but she was surprised by the one in the basement of the Palace. It resembled the human hospitals before the great war with stark white walls, tile flooring, and ample lighting. It was also comfortably heated.

For some reason, when the men discussed the cells, she had pictured a cold, dirty, dark place where they held prisoners. Any human in the forest would have found this place a practical mansion compared to the caves in which they dwelled.

Ahrkyn walked on her right, Ahdeben her left, with Ihsander bringing up the rear. She didn't need to look back to know he was looking anywhere but at her butt. After spending two hours with him putting so much distance between them when the Shifters had first appeared, she had no doubt he was probably staring at the back of her head or over her head at the hallway before them.

They walked for a while, turning down various hallways, before they slowed to a stop in front of a cell that contained a fairly comfortable looking, yet small, bed, a kitchenette with a table and small refrigerator, and a privacy wall where she assumed sat a toilet and possibly a shower.

Yep. Much better conditions than she had experienced the majority of her life.

The man raised his head from his perch on the edge of the bed and surprise entered his eyes when he spotted Valdis. Dark blond hair hung in tangles around his face, his brown eyes were so dark they were almost black, and his body was thin yet sinewy and held the strength of one who barely restrained the animal living within his skin.

He glanced at each man, then back to Valdis, straightening his back and pushing to his feet.

"There is no way you're the executioner," he said.

His voice was gravelly from lack of use. She'd heard the prisoners had refused to speak after the first night they were captured.

Yet he'd spoken to her. Granted, it was more an observation than anything useful to Ahdlai.

"My name is Valdis. I am mated to the head of the Royal guard. But…" She looked to Ahdeben. "Are there any chairs down here? This feels awkward."

He sighed like she'd put him out, but sought out a stool for her to lower onto. The Shape-Shifter pulled his bed closer to the bars and sat across from her.

That was promising. He had made an effort to move closer to either hear her out or speak with her. Either way, she might have been able to make some headway with the situation without anyone being hurt.

"I didn't grow up here. I've only been here a little over a month. I grew up in the forest and the caves with the humans."

His eyes narrowed and his nostrils flared as he scented the air. "You're not human."

"I'm not. I'm a Fae halfling."

"Why would an Elven king allow a Fae halfling to reside within his town? Fairies hate the Elves."

"I haven't lived with any member of the Fae population since I was young. I have no hate in my heart for anyone."

The man studied her, his brows pinched together, his eyes narrowed. Then his gaze moved to the men flanking her on all sides.

"They think I'm going to hurt you?"

Valdis shook her head. "I'm newly mated. It was the only way to keep my mate calm."

He nodded as though it made complete sense to him. They must have a similar Bond in their species.

"I told you my name. Any chance you'll tell me yours?"

The man looked to Ahdeben, Ahrkyn, and Ihsander, uncertainty in his eyes.

"I promise you they're not here to harm you. Have you been treated well since you were brought down here?"

"I'm being held prisoner."

Valdis made a point of looking around him and into his cell. "Other than the bars and lack of freedom, it sure seems a lot more comfortable than anything you and I have experienced in the forest."

After a few seconds, a small smile tilted up his lips and he nodded. "Yes, I've been treated well."

"No one has harassed you, beaten you, coerced you in any way?" He shook his head.

"You can trust me. I'm here to help."

After a moment, he leaned back a little and scratched at the heavy stubble that was bordering on a beard covering the lower half of his face.

"Idris," he said.

She had to fight from looking at one of the men around her. She was surprised he'd told her that much. She was doubly surprised he had said it in front of those he saw as his captors. Technically, they were.

"I was told you were recruited by the *Ihllr* to test our boundaries. They say you told them your Pack only agreed because they offered you supplies."

Again, he looked to the men around her.

"I don't suppose we could get some privacy," she said, turning to look at the Prince.

It took him a few moments, but he nodded for Ahdeben to join him. "Ihsander stays."

That was better than she expected. She truly believed the Prince would demand they stay by her side until she was finished speaking with Idris. But she wasn't there to interrogate him, only to learn more about him and help him see the truth about Ahdlai.

She waited until their footsteps sounded far enough away, then glanced back at Ihsander. He rolled his eyes, but backed up until his back was against the wall and leaned with his arms crossed over his chest.

"What did they offer you?" she asked, keeping her voice low.

"Are my men still alive?"

"They are alive and held in a cell identical to yours," Ihsander answered.

Valdis hadn't thought to ask that of anyone before coming downstairs.

Idris scratched his growing beard and lifted a leg to cross an ankle over the other knee.

"Food. They offered enough food to keep my Pack fed. We have pups – kids. We have families there. And if you truly lived out there, you know how hard it gets during the colder months to find enough to fill a belly."

"I do. We were occasionally able to grow crops during the summer, but it was rare we were able to see the harvest through to the end of the season before being discovered by the *Ihllr* elves or other groups."

"Those groups being the bloodsuckers?" Idris asked with mirth bright in his eyes.

"Yes. Vampires preyed on us when the sun set. We moved. A lot."

"Yeah. I know the feeling."

"You understand there's a slim chance the *Ihllr* will follow through with their promise, right?"

Idris sighed and dropped his head like it was too heavy for his neck. "We had our fears. But I didn't know what else to do to keep my Pack alive."

"You're the leader?"

"I'm their Alpha," Idris said.

"Where is your Pack? How many of you are there?"

Idris suddenly looked uncomfortable, and she feared she was pushing too hard.

"You don't have to tell me where they're located. I completely understand. But will you tell me how many are in your Pack? How many need to be fed?"

"There are twenty-six adults and eighteen children."

Wow. Eighteen children. She knew from experience the adults always ensured the younger ones were fed first. Trying to find enough food for forty-four people would be nearly impossible.

"If the King sent you back to your Pack with enough food to feed your people for the week, could we earn your trust?"

"What would we need to do in return to earn the food?"

Valdis shrugged. "Nothing. Don't join the *Ihllr* in attacking us. There is no reason we can't be allies. No reason we can't work together."

She hoped she wasn't overstepping the line again. She had no idea whether the King would be amenable to sending that much food with someone they'd been holding as prisoner.

But if such a small gesture would sway the Shape-Shifters to avoid their alliance with the *Ihllr*, it was worth the risk.

Jhelan nearly wore a hole in the floor with the amount of pacing he'd done since Valdis had been escorted from the dining room and down into the holding cells.

"It's been too long. Something's wrong."

"You must calm yourself, Jhelan," Queen Ahlmeda said from her seat in one of the many couches filling the living area. "Your brands would tell you if she were in danger. Have you felt anything that would cause you alarm?"

No. He hadn't. He'd felt surprise. He'd felt excitement. But no anxiety or fear.

"My mate was the same way in the beginning. You must learn to trust her. I believe she's proven herself to be a fierce warrior, despite her size. I've been told she was barely conscious when you found her, yet she attempted to fight you off with a stick?"

He huffed a laugh at the memory. "It was a fallen branch, but no thicker than her arm."

She nodded as though he had proven her point. "She's a bright woman. Intelligent and strong. Mother Universe would not send you someone so different from yourself. She knows who would best complement each of us and has sent you the best life partner you could wish for."

"I hadn't wished for a partner at all," he admitted.

Jhelan rolled his head, popping the tight joints in his neck. He hadn't trained nearly as much since Valdis's arrival, yet he constantly carried the weight of a newly mated Elf on his shoulders. His only desire was to care for her, to keep her safe, to keep her well fed and out of harm's way.

Yet she was currently downstairs speaking to the same men who had sought a way through their walls to help the enemy infiltrate Ahdlai. They had labelled themselves the enemy the moment they agreed to work with the plight of Elven existence. More than only Elves. The *Ihllr* was a plight on all living creatures, human and otherwise.

"Elabeth," Queen Ahlmeda called out.

The woman who had served the Royal Family a majority of her life, starting long before Jhelan was born, hurried into the room.

"Yes, Your Highness," she said with a bow of the head.

"Bring some wine. Jhelan is in desperate need."

"Yes, Your Highness," Elabeth said before hurrying from the room.

"Your nerves are annoying me," the Queen explained. "I figured a little alcohol might loosen you up a tad."

Jhelan couldn't hold back the laughter that barked from his mouth. He had grown up beside Ahrkyn, had thought of the Queen as a mother figure until he was old enough to understand her role in the region.

But when there were no prying eyes or ears, they tended to fall back into the role of mother and son rather than Queen and head of the Royal guard.

"I assume you are more than ready to return to your duties. The others have continued the perimeter checks and small battles when the enemy infiltrates our land, but my son tells me you have begged to return since your mate arrived."

He had. And now he couldn't stand the thought of leaving her side for the hours and sometimes days it took to complete his mission.

As much training as she'd received, she could hold her own in smaller battles, but when the *Vhtir* guard were outnumbered, they had to rely on their magic to ensure they came out the victor. Valdis had no magic. She could only rely on her sword.

"Yes. I am," he lied.

The Queen narrowed her eyes. Then a slow smile stretched across her beautiful face.

"You have never been able to lie. Not to me. You don't wish to leave your mate's side."

Jhelan sighed and dropped onto a couch across from where she sat.

"I don't. And that makes me feel like a traitor."

"You are not a traitor, Jhelan. You have served my family and this region since you were old enough to lift a sword. No. It's simply the Bond. It took years for the King to be willing to leave my side to confer with other leaders in the area. I won't tell you the need to be near your mate will disappear, but the urgency will fade with time."

As he ran her words through his mind, the brands covering his arm began to throb as his mate grew closer.

Finally. He knew he had nothing to fear. The man was locked securely behind bars and the King had sent Jhelan's closest friends with her, including the Prince.

It took a few moments from the time he felt her moving through the basement until the time he heard her soft footsteps ascending the stairs, but he forced himself to stay seated while he waited for word of her conversation with the Shape-Shifter.

Elabeth appeared with two glasses of wine and set the bottle on the table between them. When she caught the sound of others approaching, she turned to the Queen.

"Shall I bring more glasses?"

"I'm not sure," Queen Ahlmeda said, her eyes narrowed. "We shall wait and see what news they bring. Could you let the King know they have finished and ask him to join us here?"

Elabeth dipped her head. "Yes, Your Highness."

Jhelan's heart began to race as his brands tingled, the throbbing growing more intense the closer Valdis got to where he waited impatiently.

He wanted to run to the stairs, meet her where she was, and sweep her into his arms. He wanted to carry her back to the home they now shared and cover her with his body and his scent. He wanted to taste every inch of her body and swallow her moans.

A pulse of lust hit him. She'd felt his desire and her body had reacted. They were truly created for each other by the Universe.

Ahrkyn appeared at the top of the stairs first, followed by Ahdeben, then Valdis, with Ihsander bringing up the rear.

The King entered the room as the foursome joined Jhelan and the Queen in the living area.

"Would he speak to you? What have you learned?"

"The guy wouldn't *stop* talking to her," Ihsander sat as he plopped his large frame onto a winged back chair.

"It wasn't like that," Valdis said.

Jhelan stood and waited for her to take a seat on one of the cushions before lowering beside her, instantly draping an arm around her shoulders to hold her tightly to his side.

"Tell me," the King said.

"His name is Idris. And what he told you earlier sounded like the truth to me. There are eighteen children living within their Pack. They were simply doing what they had to to feed their families."

"Where are they located?" the King asked.

"I didn't push the subject. But I offered a solution that I hope you will approve."

"You said eighteen children. How many adults?" the King asked.

Jhelan looked down at his mate.

"Twenty-six. I didn't ask how many males or females."

The King nodded, his look pensive.

"What solution did you offer?"

"We release him and send enough food to feed his Pack for the week. I believe it will show we are not the enemy. A show of good faith. And I told him all we asked in return was for the Pack to refuse to work with the *Ihllr* and to call off any further surveillance on our people."

Jhelan's heart warmed at her use of the word *our*. She truly felt as though she were a part of this region, of this town, and of his life.

"Do you believe he'll hold to his end of the bargain?" King Nhaeem asked.

"I believe I would have done nearly anything to ensure my Clan was fed during the times we struggled in the wild. I don't think I would have worked with those assholes, the *Ihllr*, but…there isn't much I haven't done to fill the bellies of my people."

The King looked first to the Queen, then Ahrkyn, then to Ihsander. "Did your gift pick up any falsehoods, any lies?"

Ihsander shook his head. "No. He was telling the truth."

"What about the others?" Ahdeben asked.

"I didn't tell him we would release all of them, only him. But I can bring him a message from you," she told the King, "or offer to release his friends when he has proven we can trust him."

"Why did he speak to you and no others?" the King asked.

"Because she is a female. A woman," the Queen answered. "I had heard rumor before that Shape-Shifter males hold women with the highest honor. They are treated with the utmost respect. Or, he may simply have found young Valdis beautiful," she teased with a wink to Valdis.

While the Queen was only joking, the possessive urge to decapitate the male in the cell grew strong.

Valdis nuzzled into his side and poked him in the ribs with an elbow.

"She's playing," she whispered, although every person in the room could hear her words.

He knew that. In his bones, he knew that. But he had no control over his emotions. He had to remind himself over and over that while he could not control his emotions, he could control his actions. And he would not rush downstairs to attack someone unprovoked.

"Release them all. Send a contingency of guard to carry the food," King Nhaeem ordered.

Valdis shook her head. "They won't guide you to where their children are. They don't know us well enough to trust us. They would rather stay down there for the rest of their lives than risk their families," she said.

How had he gotten so lucky? He hadn't wanted a mate, yet the Universe sent him exactly the person he needed. Mother Universe sent him the person who made Jhelan a better person.

"Enough food to feed forty-four people for a week is too much for three men to carry," Jhelan said.

"I'll go with them. We can load up Little Dove or hook a wagon to her."

"Absolutely not. And don't look at me like that," Jhelan said when his mate turned a glare on him. "You have been training. Yes. You have become a fierce fighter. But you're still a small woman. And there are still a lot of enemies out there and others who would feast on your body, your blood, or your flesh."

"Don't you think I know that?" she said, turning her body to look fully into Jhelan's face. "I've lived out there my whole life. And please don't forget I've only known you a month. That means I was able to survive without you all that time. I know where to hide, I know when to run. I'm not stupid."

Damn it. She had once again thrown that word in his face.

"Would they allow at least one other guard to accompany you?" the Queen asked.

"How is that any better?" Jhelan asked.

Jhelan had a long and deep relationship with the Royal family. But Queen Ahlmeda was still the Queen of Ahdlai and Jhelan was still nothing more than a guard.

Her dark brows slowly lowered as her head dipped enough for Jhelan to feel a spark of fear. Ahlmeda was rumored to have gifts and magic that could end a man's life in a blink of an eye or cause him to go mad. He had never seen those gifts in action, but didn't want to be the target, either.

"I thought since you are adamant to be near your mate, you could escort her through the woods with the Shape-Shifters." Her eyes took on a hint of glow as her anger began to grow. "Or shall I send another?"

The room was so quiet one could hear a mouse in the walls. All eyes bounced between the Queen and Jhelan. Even the King remained quiet as he allowed his mate to handle this particular situation.

They had been mated for over a century and had fought and won several battles against various enemies. They could communicate with nothing more than a glance. They trusted each other implicitly.

"I'll ask if he would allow myself and Jhelan to accompany them to help carry the food. But you must promise not to send others to follow. They'll pick up your scent and any headway I might have made will be lost," Valdis said.

The glow in Queen Ahlmeda's eyes slowly faded as she nodded.

"Speak to him," the King said. "If he agrees, I will release them all and send the food. But remind them if they betray us, there will be consequences far worse than starvation."

Chapter Fourteen

Valdis could feel so many emotions rushing through her, coming from herself and from her mate. She sat atop Little Dove with a small wagon hitched to her to drag along the larger items.

Jhelan had wanted to bring his own mare, but she thought it might be better for him to stay on foot with the released prisoners. It made them appear equal.

The men were apprehensive about Jhelan accompanying them, but acquiesced to Valdis's requests. She reminded them she would have to return to town alone if her mate didn't join them.

They had offered to escort her back, but she saw no reason for them to make so many trips.

"Why would your King be willing to part with so much?" Idris asked.

"He is your King, too," Jhelan grumbled.

Valdis shot him a glare, but he was looking into the woods, his body tight and his senses on alert for any sign of trouble.

"We don't follow anyone's leader. We're free. As is anyone who dwells within the woods."

"The woods are still part of the region of Ahdlai. Therefore, you are still held to the same standards as those who have chosen to live within the towns," Jhelan said.

Idris looked over his shoulder and grunted. But there was no further argument.

Valdis was thankful for that. The last thing they needed on their trip was constant bickering between themselves. They were not enemies. They were all the same, simply trying to survive in the world after the humans had destroyed it so long ago.

"How far is your home?" Valdis asked after a long stretch of silence.

"Another few hours."

"Great," Jhelan muttered.

She turned her head and glared down at her mate. "You could always return home and wait for me to come back."

His attitude wasn't doing anyone any good.

He snorted, as if the thought was ludicrous.

She knew he wouldn't leave her there in the woods, especially not with three strange men.

They took a few breaks to allow Little Dove to sip from streams or creeks while they snacked on a few things Jhelan had packed in a satchel.

"Is your King nearly as good as you portray?" one of the men asked.

"Yes. He is. I had only requested the release of one of you as a show of good faith. It was his idea to allow all three of you to return home," Valdis said.

"We return without our fallen Pack brothers," the other said.

"I'm sorry for that. They were given a proper funeral and burial. You have my word."

"We now have to return to their mates, to their children with the news that each of them will not be coming home."

"Perhaps you shouldn't have attacked the wall," Jhelan said.

He leaned against a tree, his head resting against the bark, as he listened to the conversation.

"We did not attack. We were merely sent to find any cracks in the armor, any easy entry points. Your guard attacked us. We fought back," Idris said.

When Jhelan opened his mouth to argue further, Valdis threw up a hand. She knew her mate would stop out of love for her. But she was surprised when all three men instantly grew quiet and lowered their eyes.

Could Queen Ahlmeda have been correct about their deference and respect for females?

"Mistakes were made. But the situation can be righted. We are not asking you to fight on our behalf. We only ask that you do not fight against us."

"We will not attack Ahdlai with the *Ihllr*," Idris said.

He raised his fist and thumped it against his chest hard enough for Valdis to wonder if it hadn't hurt.

Each Shape-Shifter did the same, raising their fists to thump them against their chests in some form of vow.

"Do they know where your Pack is located?" Valdis asked.

Idris nodded.

"You'll need to move. You know that. When you refuse to fight with them, they'll attack and kill your people. I watched them slaughter my own Clan not long ago."

"I know. When we've arrived home, we'll make the preparations to move on. Such has been our way of life since the beginning, long before the world as we knew it changed."

"Will you need help? Would you like me to ask some guard members to help move your people to another location?"

Jhelan made a sound of protest, but Valdis ignored it. She had been a nomad, as well. She knew how difficult it was to leave a home and start over somewhere new. She knew how hard it was to find somewhere safe, somewhere she could lie her head at night without fear of being taken or murdered in her sleep.

Honestly, it hadn't been until she'd begun to sleep in Jhelan's bed that she had slept a night through without waking at every sound, fearing her Clan had been found by another group.

"I would prefer the rest of your people not learn of our new location," Idris said.

"Yet you know where we are," Jhelan said.

Idris frowned over his shoulder and looked at Jhelan like he'd said the most ridiculous thing in the world. In a way, he had.

"You're in the center of Ahdlai. Your homes are positioned outside the walls of the Palace. How would we not know where you're located?"

The other three chuckled.

Jhelan grumbled under his breath, cursing the Shape-Shifters. Valdis couldn't help the smile that bloomed on her face. Now that the men were out of the cells and back in the wilderness, their personalities were shining through and their postures were no longer rigid.

What Jhelan either didn't realize or didn't want to was how much he would like these men if he were to see them as regular people trying to survive.

Because they *hadn't* attacked the Palace. They had passed so many houses and not one person had been harmed, not one item had gone missing. Had they not been spotted by the guards walking the perimeter of the fence and staying vigilant in the towers, everyone in Ahdlai might have remained unaware of the trespassers.

Idris hadn't exaggerated when he'd said their Pack was a few more hours away. Valdis's foot had healed, but she was glad she hadn't spent half the day on it as she made her way through the forest, the thick brush, and fallen limbs.

The sounds of children's laughter met her ears and her heart burst with joy and nostalgia. That was her once. That was how her Clan had sounded once. They were the sounds of life and happiness. The sound of freedom unlike most would ever know.

"Idris?" a female called out. "Idris!"

A woman with a dark braid reaching her waist raced past those who milled about or worked on their settlement and made a beeline for him.

He dropped what he carried and met her halfway, his arms closing around her, his lips crashing down on hers.

His mate. He was reunited with his mate.

We now have to return to their mates, to their children with the news that each of them will not be coming home.

Valdis and Jhelan would be witness to the bone deep grief of learning news of the death of a loved one. She had seen it more times than she would like to admit in her long life.

Had Jhelan ever had to deliver that kind of news to his people? Most were not mated for life. Most did not have a Bond such as the one she shared with Jhelan or the King shared with his Queen. Most only paired long enough to conceive and deliver a child before returning to their own homes and their own lives.

They hung back as the three reunited with their Pack, updating everyone about the losses of those who hadn't returned.

There were tears, there were bellows of grief, children clung to their mothers as they held each other and cried.

And there were so many accusatory glares in Valdis's and Jhelan's direction.

She held their stares. She wouldn't look away. She didn't mind if they aimed their anger at her. It had been her new family, her new people who had killed the men who would no longer be with their Pack.

Jhelan's emotions poured through their brand. He was uncomfortable. He was concerned. But the biggest emotion was…guilt.

He hadn't been a part of killing anyone, yet it had been the men he'd trained who had executed those they'd believed to be there to infiltrate the city of Ahdlai and harm its people.

"The King of Ahdlai sent food for the Pack," Idris announced when the tears began to slow. "He released us and sent all of this in hopes we don't join the *Ihllr* in attacking their region."

"Why shouldn't we? They killed several good men," a Shifter nearby said.

Jhelan moved closer to Valdis. He placed a hand on her hip and moved her slightly behind him in case there was a fight. The two of them were far outnumbered. With his magic being unhelpful in this kind of situation and her magic being nonexistent, there was no chance they would come out the victors.

And Valdis had no desire to inflict any more pain on these people. They had endured enough.

"They are trying to buy our allegiance with food," another male said.

"If we take the food, we will be enslaved to them," another said.

Valdis held up her hands, palms out. "I know none of you know me or my mate. My name is Valdis. Until a month ago, I lived in the forest like you. I lived among the humans. The *Ihllr* Elves located my Clan and slaughtered them. I assume they're all dead, although the women of childbearing age might have been taken as breeders. The food we have brought is not an agreement to work *with* or *for* the *Vhtir* of Ahdlai. It is simply a show of good faith. And I'm sorry for those you have lost. I know that pain all too well."

Idris moved closer until he was nearly standing at her side. "I was not held in poor conditions. It was more comfortable than out here. I was able to use the toilet in privacy."

That earned a few chuckles.

"It is true they killed a few of our men. But they were unaware of our objective. They had received word from an ally that we had agreed to work with their enemy to attack and overthrow their King. They thought they were under attack."

"Bull shit," another said.

A ripple of power made the hair on Valdis's arms stand on end. The one who had spoken out immediately dropped his eyes and tilted his head as if he were exposing his neck for slaughter. A show of submission?

"We will not fight with the *Ihllr*. We are under no obligation to come to the aid of the *Vhtir* or Ahdlai. We will accept this food. We will move our camp immediately. And we will allow these two to return to their homes without interference."

There were a few grumbles, but no one outwardly disagreed with their Alpha.

Jhelan and Valdis helped unload the rest of the food from the cart and backed away. Jhelan's emotions were all over the place and feeding directly down their Bonding brand.

He needed to calm down. She had been fine, sad for these people, but unafraid. But with his rush of fear and misplaced anger, she was having a hard time discerning her emotions from his.

"If you need anything else, you know where to find us," she said.

"*You* won't know where to find *us*," Idris promised.

She nodded her head in agreement and climbed atop of Little Dove with a hoist from Jhelan.

"Do you want to join me up here?"

"She can't handle the weight of both of us. I should have brought a bigger horse and left your pony at home," Jhelan said.

He couldn't help the constant urge to check behind them to make sure none of the Shape-Shifters followed them with the intent to attack.

Yet he couldn't see them harming Valdis. He had witnessed the way they had spoken to her, the way they barely met her eyes when she spoke, had witnessed the way they had treated the women in their Pack.

"Any chance we'll make it home before the sun sets?" she asked.

He could feel her trying to force her calmness through their Bond. And loved her for her.

"Doubtful. But I won't camp out here with you. Not without more members of the guard present."

She had no desire to camp outside, either. While she had grown accustomed to it, she was also used to sleeping with some form of shelter such as a cave. They would have to sleep under the trees, their bodies sprawled on a pelt spread on the forest floor. And extremely vulnerable to an attack by those who prowled and hunted at night.

"We should have brought more snacks along," she said.

Jhelan tilted his head back to look up at his mate. Was she truly hungry or was she attempting small talk?

"I have more deer jerky or some fruit in the satchel if you're hungry."

"I'm craving something sweet. What did you bring?"

He pulled the satchel from the side of the saddle and rifled through. She nodded when he presented an apple.

And then they once again walked in silence. Well, she rode. He was mildly surprised she hadn't chosen to walk beside him. It saved him yet another argument for the day. He would love her at his side, but preferred she not push her body too far. She was fully healed, but it would only take a twist of an ankle to reinjure her foot.

Then again, that would put them back to where they began when he was able to cradle her against his chest as he carried her everywhere.

But she had hated that. Hated being dependent on others. Hated not being able to get up and do whatever she wanted when she wanted.

He understood that. It was the biggest reason he'd never wanted to mate with a female. Why he'd been so resistant to Ahrkyn thrusting her on him and declaring her Jhelan's responsibility.

Jhelan could no longer remember a life before Valdis. He could no longer imagine his life without her.

"You sure she can't hold us both? We could get her at a canter and get home faster," Valdis said.

There was a tone to her voice. A teasing tone. Seconds later, obvious lust blasted through his brands.

Nope. That pony wouldn't hold the weight of both Jhelan and Valdis. But the ground sure would.

Pulling on the lead, he pulled the horse to a stop, gripped his mate by the waist, and pulled her from the saddle.

She squealed and giggled as he gripped her thighs and forced her to wrap them around his waist.

Since her foot was healed, she could now wear pants beneath the tunic. Pity. Because they would have to take time he didn't want to wait to remove them so he could plunge deep inside her tight heat.

As he walked them toward the shelter of a tree with budding leaves, he slanted his lips over hers, reveled in the velvety sweetness of her mouth.

Her breath huffed out of her when her back hit a tree. He hadn't meant to walk them that far.

"I'm sorry," he said, pulling away to look into her eyes and ensure himself she was okay.

"I'm fine," she said. She gripped his head by two handfuls of hair and pulled him back so she could go back to kissing him.

Dropping to his knees, he set her down gently so he could peel her pants from her legs and unbuckle his pants. He pushed them over his ass only low enough to free his cock, then lowered over Valdis as she dropped onto her back.

Her knees were parted and she held her arms open, inviting him to her, begging her to connect with her.

And each time they had made love, it was exactly that – a connection unlike any he had ever experienced. It was far more than sex. It was deeper. Like their souls entwined, like they had formed a true alliance between themselves and their species in that moment.

Positioning the head of his cock to her entrance, he watched as her eyes closed when he slowly entered her inch by inch. He no longer had to take it slowly or carefully with her. She would raise her hips to meet him thrust for thrust, chasing her own release as he struggled to hold back his own.

It was always that way. He needed her to find ecstasy before he allowed himself that pleasure. He would be even more content if he could push her toward two or more before finishing inside of her.

He hadn't thought he wanted an heir. It hadn't bothered him that because of their halfling blood they could never conceive. But as pressure built and he teetered on the edge, he wondered what kind of mother she would have been, what kind of father he would have been.

Jhelan needed to push those thoughts out of his head. There was no reason to dwell on something neither of them had any control over. This was their life. And he was filled with joy that he got to spend the next few centuries of his existence with a woman like Valdis by his side.

As long as they survived the attack planned by the *Ihllr* and any recruits they could convince to attempt to annihilate Ahdlai and its people.

Chapter Fifteen

Valdis pulled her arms over her head and stretched. It had been another two weeks since the Shape-Shifters had been released to return to their families, two weeks since she and Jhelan had helped them carry enough food to their people to last at least a week…two weeks since she and Jhelan had made love in the woods with the darkening sky overhead.

Once they had finished, they picked up their pace and hurried back to town to avoid running into any vampires or other nocturnal creatures who would attack two people out alone. Regardless of how well armed and trained either of them were.

Jhelan was absent from the bed, his spot already cooled as she ran her hand over the sheets.

The scent of food wafted throughout the house and compelled Valdis's legs to drop to the floor and rush her into the kitchen.

Since beginning her training, she was perpetually hungry. She now understood why the guard members were always looking for something to snack on or hurrying to the table at meal times. She constantly burned so many calories. But her body was the strongest it had ever been.

Not only did she have regular meals, but she was being taught to use her body as a weapon as well as whatever tool she held in her hands.

"Good morning," he said without turning to look at her.

They had explored the brands linking them in the past couple weeks. They couldn't pinpoint the exact location of the other, but were guided in their direction. And they had both practiced closing off their emotions to the other as well as seeking help through their Bond.

Through that practice, they had figured out that Valdis could let him know from any distance that she was in danger, or whether she was able to continue fighting without his aid.

That would come in extremely handy should the *Ihllr* truly attack as Ahdlai had been warned. Jhelan would not need to constantly check on her while fighting and risk being hurt or killed during the momentary distraction.

"I'm starving," she said as she took a seat.

He chuckled, the throaty sound doing all kinds of delicious things to her body.

That was something else they had discovered during their experimentations – they could feel each other's lust so much that it instantly made the other react. At no point could either hide how much they wanted each other. Not that they would have any need to hide something like that.

"You've been working hard," Jhelan said.

He plated the food and carried it to the table. She scarfed it down so quickly she wasn't sure whether she actually tasted anything.

Jhelan simply shook his head with a smile as he took his time. He'd had plenty of time to get used to the work she had begun only weeks ago. But she had seen him devour enough food to know he got just as famished.

"I have to return to my duties today," he announced.

They knew the day would come when he was no longer at her side day in and day out. Yet knowing made it no better. She would miss him. Because of the duties assigned to the guard, he could be gone hours or days. It was the fact he could be gone days that bothered her.

An alert went off throughout the town, letting everyone know someone was approaching.

Valdis didn't bother with the battle armor she'd been fitted with by the seamstress, but she did don pants and a clean tunic before grabbing her sword and following Jhelan through the front door.

Other guards were emerging from their own homes or jogging from the Palace to see whether there was a need to sound the alarm.

A man she had briefly seen once ambled into view, four women flanking him on all sides. This was no ordinary man. Not a human. Not an Elf.

He stood at least seven feet tall, maybe taller. His face was rugged and terrifying, yet his eyes held a kindness she wouldn't expect on a creature such as he. His lips peeled back in what she assumed was a smile and revealed what could only be described as long, pointy fangs that hung over his bottom lip.

An ogre. She had never seen one with her own two eyes and had wondered if they weren't made up to convince children to stay close to their parents.

All in all, he was terrifying. Had Jhelan reacted any differently, she would have assumed this was a monster sent by their enemy. But he was relaxed, the emotions pouring through their brand were of familiarity and curiosity.

Prince Ahrkyn jogged past the others and held out an arm. The giant clasped Ahrkyn's forearm and nodded.

"What has the Coven decided?" the Prince asked.

"We will stand by your side. Some have chosen to stay back, but others will be arriving soon. So please ask your guard to refrain from harming them. We heard what happened with the Shape-Shifters."

No one bothered to look the least bit remorseful. They'd had no idea what was happening and reacted to what they thought was a threat. Those killed along the wall had fought back. But Valdis had been told one man was killed when he'd refused to speak and disrespected the King. While the manner of death was described, the method was never revealed to her.

"How many will stand with us?" Ahrkyn asked.

The ogre looked to his companions. "There are eight more following a few hours, possibly a day behind us."

Twelve witches, an ogre, and the Royal guard. Would it be enough?

"Any more word on the *Ihllr's* recruiting efforts?"

The ogre grinned wide. "Only that the Shape-Shifters will no longer fight with them. They sent word that they will remain neutral. Then they disappeared."

Good. The Pack had moved as they said they would. Hopefully, they would remain unfound by the *Ihllr*.

"How many will you have?" the ogre asked. His eyes flitted to Valdis, then did a double take. "My apologies. I am Brizio. These are my companions. I would tell you their names, but they have not told me." He placed a hand over his heart and bowed.

"I am Valdis. Mate to Jhelan."

Brizio's face lit up with joy and surprise as he turned to Jhelan and nodded.

For such a ginormous, intimidating creature, he behaved as though he were the jolliest giant to ever exist.

"We have sixty members of the Royal guard, though many are spread around the territory."

"Sixty-one," Valdis corrected.

Ahrkyn frowned at her then looked to Jhelan with raised brows.

"I've learned to avoid arguing with her. I never win."

"Okay. Sixty-one. But we're still spread out. There are thirty – thirty-one members stationed here at all times to protect the King and Queen."

"And yourself, I assume," Brizio said.

It wasn't an accusation or a jab, merely an observation.

"When needed, yes, myself as well."

"And your mate will be fighting?" he asked Jhelan.

Jhelan sighed heavily and Valdis felt the frustration rush through their brands.

"She is strong willed. If she chooses to fight alongside us, then I can't stop her."

"I will stay close to your mate. I will not let anything happen to her."

Valdis felt her own surprise the moment Jhelan's flared.

"So far, we've heard nothing more from the *Ihḷlr*," Ahrkyn said. "Let's hope they've been dissuaded by the Shifters' refusal to join them." He waved a hand toward the castle. "Please. Come inside. You must be hungry after your travels. We have plenty for everyone."

Brizio placed a hand over his heart again and followed Ahrkyn inside along with his silent witch companions.

"Do witches not speak?" Valdis asked when they were all out of earshot.

Or so she thought.

One of the women looked back and directly at Valdis and winked before turning back around.

"I've had very little interaction with their kind. We once believed them to be humans who'd learned the use of herbs. But from stories that have spread through the years, I believe them to be of the paranormal or supernatural race. Either way, their gifts will help if we're outnumbered," Jhelan said.

She turned toward him and looked up into his face. "You still have to head out? Will they still insist you return to your duties?"

Jhelan nodded. "It's my job. And we'll be able to detect anyone moving toward the town. Ahrkyn and Ihsander will remain behind. And the ogre and his friends will be here to watch over you, as well."

She screwed up her face. "You think I'm worried about myself? I'm worried about you, Jhelan. There will be plenty of people here, even if the ogre and witches left, even if Ahrkyn and Ihsander went with you. But there will only be a handful of you out there. What if all of this was a ploy to begin picking off the guard one by one so attacking the Palace will be easy."

"You have an extremely active imagination, *khaere*."

Valdis moved closer. "What does that mean? You've called me that before. But I've never thought to ask you what you were calling me?"

"It's an old Elven word. It's like saying my love, or my dearest one."

Warmth unfurled in her chest like a cat stretching after a nap in the sun. He had called her that pretty early on, indicating how deeply his emotions had run for her.

He had told her once that he thought he had begun to fall in love with her the moment she lifted that fallen branch and swung it at him. She tried to think back to the moment she realized her heart was turning from gratitude to love.

There was no one moment. All the little things he had done for her, even when he was surly and grouchy. The way he had been so careful and gentle with her, the way he'd brought the pony so she wouldn't have to rely on someone to carry her around the property or into the woods.

The way he put her life and happiness before his own.

It had all combined to form a love so deep and true she sometimes wondered if she was simply in the middle of a dream and feared waking to a reality without him.

"When do you leave?" she asked.

He draped an arm around her shoulders and guided her back to the house they shared. Their home.

"Once everyone has finished their breakfast and changed into their battle gear, we'll have to leave."

"If I whined or pouted, would it convince you to allow me to tag along?"

"No. But it would be cute," he teased.

He opened the front door and swatted her on the butt as she walked ahead of him.

"You wouldn't want to join us. Trust me. With a few rare exceptions, it's usually pretty boring. Just walking around the woods, checking the perimeters, watching for any signs of trespassers."

"But you never bother the humans?"

He shook his head as he began to lay out his leather vest and breeches. "Nah. They are of no threat to us. We're aware they steal from town, but they cause no harm to the residents. We know it's a struggle, and will continue to welcome any who choose to stay within the town rather than merely survive out there."

After he pulled his breeches up his legs, she watched him pull his undershirt over his head and found herself once again mesmerized by the perfection and beauty of his body.

He groaned and narrowed his eyes on her.

"I can feel your arousal. I need to leave. Calm yourself, woman."

"I can't help it. I mean, look at you."

"I'd rather look at you."

He bent to pick up his leather battle vest, but pressed a kiss to her lips as he passed.

Valdis took the vest from his hands and held it up, waiting for him to slide his arms through, then worked quickly, tying the leather straps along the front. They had helped each other each time they'd donned the gear. She could help him prepare in her sleep.

"You'll be careful?" she asked, her fingers gripping the vest.

Jhelan rested his hands on her hips. "I have someone to return to, someone waiting for me. You have given me something to look forward to, *khaere*. A reason to take less risks. A reason to be careful. I will always return to you."

Tilting his head, he slanted his mouth over hers and pressed a heartwarmingly gentle caress to her lips.

She sighed in contentment. More than contentment. She was happy. For the first time in her life, she could truly say she knew the meaning of happiness, the feeling of pure love and joy.

And it was all because of the man who stole her breath with every touch.

"Your mate has changed you," Ahdeben said.

"How so?" Jhelan asked.

Ahdeben glanced at him from atop his steed and shook his head. "I don't know. You're just…different. Antsy. Impatient."

"Because I want to return home to my mate."

"You want to return home to get your mate in bed," Ahdeben teased.

Jhelan chuckled. "That, too."

They walked in silence a few more moments.

"Do you trust the ogre?" Ahdeben asked.

"Ihsander detected no deception. I trust his gift."

"The witches are creepy, though," Ahdeben said. "Have you heard them utter a single word?"

"They only arrived shortly before we left. We are new to each other. Perhaps they'll warm up to the others in our absence."

"Or perhaps they are actually ghosts and don't speak."

"Ghosts?" Jhelan asked.

Ahdeben visibly shivered. "They appear to float when they move. The cloaks they don cover their feet and most of their bodies. What's to say they aren't spirits here to haunt us."

Jhelan sighed and shook his head. "I told my mate this morning she had an active imagination. I now realize yours far surpasses hers."

"Why? Did she think they were ghosts, too?"

"No," Jhelan said. "She fears the *Ihllr* or their minions are out here in wait, hoping to pick off the guard in smaller groupings so an attack on Ahdlai would be easier."

Ahdeben was quiet for a few moments before he turned to look at Jhelan. "That isn't too far-fetched."

He looked around as if there were a threat hiding around every bush, every tree. The two of them or one of the four guards on horses following behind would have sensed, scented, or heard someone if they were hiding nearby.

Although they hadn't detected the Shape-Shifters. Were there others like them who could mask their scents, keep the Elven guards from detecting their presence?

That thought was unnerving. Not because he feared an ambush, but because Ahdlai could be razed and the inhabitants killed without a single person sounding the alarm.

His mate was there. She was in Ahdlai. Without him.

"Calm yourself," Ahdeben said. "I'm not Bonded to you yet can feel your tension. Your mate will, as well. You'll scare her for no reason."

He hated when Ahdeben was right. Rather, he hated when he was called out on his behavior. His anxiety would feed down their brands and she would fear he was in danger. He could close the link as they had practiced, but then he wouldn't feel if she needed him.

It would take him far too long to get to her side if she was in danger. He had to trust those left behind to ensure no one laid a finger on his beautiful mate.

"I like her," Ahdeben blurted out of the blue.

"I can tell. It appears everyone respects her."

"It's more than that. She...she makes you better. She makes everyone a little better. She makes the trainees work harder. And she is a good diplomat. She would make a good Queen someday."

"Yet that will never happen. I'm merely a guard. Not of royal blood. She is not Ahrkyn's mate. Or was that what you were getting at?"

Ahdeben rolled his eyes, reminding Jhelan so much of Valdis when she was annoyed.

"Did I at any point mention allowing Ahrkyn to Claim your mate? I'm not sure such is possible with a Bond blessed by Mother Universe.

All I'm saying is she is strong. You don't need to worry about her in your absence. I think anyone who dares to challenge her in a fight, whether with words or weapons, would regret it instantly."

The guard behind them grumbled sounds of agreement while others chuckled.

She had bartered for the freedom of the Shifters who'd been held in the cells below. She had bargained with the King to send food to their people. She'd healed and fought to strengthen her body. She had trained her tight little ass off.

Valdis truly was a warrior. A tiny warrior, but a warrior nonetheless.

As Jhelan tuned into his link to check on his mate, a scent hit his nose the same moment his weak sense of precognition warned him someone was near.

Holding up his hand, he brought the group of guards to a halt.

Ahdeben's brows drew together as his nostrils flared. He caught it, as well. There was someone out here, someone who was moving to their left. Behind them. To the right.

They were circling the group.

Jhelan gave the signal for those in the rear to turn toward the back and those in the middle to face outward. They had done the same formation more times than he could count.

Another scent. Then another.

They were unfamiliar, but they had been warned by Brizio his Coven friends would be joining Ahdlai. Could the witches have arrived early?

Jhelan moved away from the group and dismounted his mare. He dropped the lead, prepared to slap her rump to get her moving if needed. All the horses knew the way home; if there was a carnivorous creature stalking the group, he didn't want to risk his horse being eaten when it had the opportunity to flee.

Pulling his sword from its sheath, he sent out his senses to try to pinpoint one of the intruders. They were still on the move and silent. The sun was high. Not vampires. The Shape-Shifters had vowed to stay neutral and avoid the fight.

Ihllr Elves? But Elves weren't known for being able to stay so far off his radar.

He glanced back at Ahdeben and the others. They looked as confused as he felt.

After one more check in with Valdis through their link to ensure all was still well back at home, he began to creep toward the strongest scent, careful to avoid fallen twigs. But he couldn't avoid the littering of dead leaves on the late spring forest floor.

His steps weren't silent, yet quieter than a human's or a wild animal's.

The scent stayed in place, yet those around him still moved. Did the intruder hear Jhelan's approach? Was he watching him slink through the brush?

Before disappearing from view, he turned back to Ahdeben to silently gesture that he was now in charge. Leather creaked as the remaining five Royal guards dismounted their horses and turned to Ahdeben for orders.

Something familiar tickled his senses, something about the scent rolling from whom he hunted. Familiar yet alien. He couldn't put his finger on it and that set his nerves on edge.

With a deep breath, he slowed his heart rate and focused on his lifelong training until his senses were razor sharp.

There. Whoever was toying with the guard was just behind that tree.

And then she wasn't.

A woman, small like Valdis, stepped into view, a smirk on her face. A glow flashed from the pupils of her eyes and Jhelan finally realized why the presence felt so familiar – this woman was a Fairy. There were Fae now encircling his guard, encircling his men.

Elves had their magic, but it was nothing compared to the Fae species. And, without knowing whether they were currently encountering Seelie or Unseelie, Jhelan kept a tight grip on his sword and stayed at the ready. He couldn't fight elemental magic with a sword, but he could incapacitate the woman with a serious injury. And as much as he didn't relish killing a woman, he would if it meant getting back to his mate alive.

"I am Jhelan, head of the Royal guard. You are trespassing on Ahdlai territory," he announced.

He would try diplomacy first. It had worked for Valdis. And he prayed to the Universe that it worked for him.

The woman continued to smirk while staring at him silently. Her hands were clasped in front of her, her long gown flowed out behind her with a breeze that ruffled her hair and stirred up leaves and brush.

"They're Fae!" Ahdeben yelled from where Jhelan had left him.

Six guard members were surrounded by an unknown number of Fairies whose magic could snuff the life out of every single one of the men. And there wasn't a damn thing anyone could do about it.

"I will only tell you once more," Jhelan said. "You are trespassing in Ahdlai territory. If you wish to seek permission to pass through, I will escort only one of you back to our King."

As Jhelan explained the rules to the woman, his brands began to burn. Not throb. Not tingle. They burned. Then a sense of panic laced with fear slammed into his heart so fast and so hard it nearly stole the breath from his lungs and knocked him on his ass.

His mate. Something was wrong with his mate. Those were her emotions, not his own. There was trouble within the town or behind the walls.

And Jhelan had no idea whether he would be able to get past this woman and to her side.

One way or another, he would get to Valdis. Even if he had to slaughter every single Fairy who got in his way.

If he could stay alive that long.

Chapter Sixteen

Valdis felt varying emotions through her link to Jhelan, but none gave her any reason to fear for his safety. He was doing what he had done for decades. He was doing what he was trained to do.

But there was still another feeling niggling at her; something felt off. She couldn't pinpoint the source of her unease, but it was there, right on the cusp of her senses.

As she walked beside Ihsander, watching the trainees run through their drills, she couldn't shake the feeling of being watched.

Turning in a circle, she looked at every tree, every bush, toward the gardens, even into the many windows in the Palace. No one was directly staring at her or intently watching the goings-on of the trainees.

"What is it?" Ihsander asked.

She turned to look into his face. His brows were pulled low. The King had asked him to accompany her to speak with the Shape-Shifters, had asked him to use his gift to detect any lies. Perhaps he had strong empathic abilities.

"I don't know," she admitted.

She couldn't put her finger on it, couldn't figure out what it was that was causing the hair on her arms and the back of her neck to bristle.

A sensation came over her. Like a wave, it rushed over her, surrounded her. She had felt it before but couldn't place it. It was from somewhere deep in her memories, a place she could not access easily.

The men in the towers suddenly called out and sounded the alarm.

Oh no. They were officially under attack and Jhelan was somewhere out where the enemy would be crossing.

The same time the alarms were sounded, she felt anxiety rise through her Bond to her mate. He was in danger.

She should have gone with him. Should have been there to back him up.

But had she gone, that would have been one less person to protect the people of Ahdlai.

Like a tidal wave, the residents poured through the gate and toward the Palace where those who were untrained or unable to fight would hide safely in the basement. It had been reinforced for prisoners, but was strong enough to protect the residents as well as the Royal Family.

Ahrkyn rushed toward her, the ogre and the witches following closely behind.

"Get inside," he ordered, jabbing a finger at her.

"Bull shit. I'm staying right here. I won't let those assholes hurt another person. Not as long as I have breath in my lungs."

She pulled the sword Jhelan had made for her from its sheath and swung it with flourish in circles, loosening her muscles in preparation for whatever was coming their way.

"If you get hurt, Jhelan will cut our throats," Ihsander said.

"Then stay at my back so I won't get hurt."

"I will stay by your side. I already made the vow to your mate. I will not let anyone hurt you," Brizio said, hand over his heart.

As big as he was, he could plow through a group of people without breaking a sweat.

The witches moved forward, waiting at either side of the gate until the last resident ran through. They used magic to close the doors, then held up their hands. A golden glow covered their skin, the iridescence coming from somewhere deep inside, as they chanted in a tone so low it was almost indiscernible, but once again, made her nerve endings tingle.

Perhaps that was why they had yet to speak to anyone. At least when she was around. Their voices were like music, urging Valdis closer while sending dread through her system at the same time.

"What are they doing?"

"Adding a barrier. It will make it harder for the enemy to crash through with brute strength," Brizio answered.

Ahrkyn ran toward one of the towers and tilted his head back. "Can you see them?"

"We see movement within the brush. It's coming from all directions. They are flanking the area, Your Highness," the guard answered.

The *Ihllr* and whoever they had convinced to join them were surrounding the residents of Ahdlai.

There were thirty guards, thirty-one counting Valdis, the ogre, and his witch companions. Their other friends had yet to arrive, but there weren't enough arriving to cause so much commotion in the surrounding forest.

They were definitely under attack.

A bellow sounded from the back of the property. A pained sound followed shortly after.

Valdis raised her eyes to Ihsander, expecting him to give her orders since he and Ahdeben had been the ones to train her.

"Stay with Brizio and the witches. Watch the gate," he ordered.

Then he took off in the direction of the obvious sounds of battle. The sounds were coming from outside the wall. Guard members were being challenged, attacked, and possibly killed.

Why hadn't everyone been brought inside? She could understand the desire to add yet one more roadblock to the attack, but those who had been assigned to remain outside would be easily outnumbered and overrun. They would be slaughtered as easily as if they were children fighting against a group of adults.

"They need to be brought inside!" she yelled at Ahrkyn. "Call the guard back inside the wall. They'll be overrun."

Ahrkyn looked to the tower. One of the men looked down, around, then shook his head. "I see none on this side."

"Brizio, take Valdis with you. Check each tower. Any members outside the wall need to be called back in immediately."

"Yes, Your Highness."

When Valdis turned to run, she was swept off her feet and into the ogre's arms. She protested and struggled to be put back on her feet at first, then stopped when she realized how much more space his legs ate than her own. They would get there in half the time with him carrying her rather than waiting for her to keep pace.

A blast of air blew her hair from her face and gave Brizio a shove forward. He stumbled, but righted himself.

Where the hell had that come from? The trees within the walls weren't swaying, there were no storm clouds in the sky. And it gave her a stronger sense of fear. It wasn't natural. It was magic. Someone with strong elemental magic had joined forces with the *Ihllr*.

And the only beings she knew with that kind of gift were the Fae, her own people.

Seelie Fairies would have no reason to attack. If she was right and the Unseelie Court had sent some of their people, there might be nothing any of them could do to win this battle.

An elemental Fae could control elements of fire, wind, earth, or water. They could easily blast the entire area with fire and keep it going with gust after gust of wind until there were no buildings and no people left behind to tell the tale.

"Hey! Prince Ahrkyn said to call them in. Any guard outside the walls need to come inside now!" she yelled to each tower they passed.

But it didn't matter whether the guard were out there to stop the intruders or not. Because someone had gotten in through another means.

People began to scream in terror as they realized there were members of the *Ihllr* and their cohorts coming from under the wall. How…

Damn it. The Fae magic. They'd removed enough of the earth for the enemy to infiltrate from behind while everyone was focused on the front gate.

"Back here!" she screamed as loud as she could.

Brizio set her on her feet then shoved her behind his big body like a living, breathing shield.

But it didn't matter. The *Ihllr* fighters began to circle the two of them, reminding her of sharks in the sea, their sneers and snarls intended to intimidate.

All it did was enrage her.

How dare these assholes interrupt the life she had built? How dare they come into this place and destroy the happiness she had finally found. How dare they come here to destroy a place that had brought nothing but safety and peace to so many.

With a battle cry, Valdis lifted her sword, pointed it at the closest opponent, then attacked.

Brizio stayed close, but he couldn't give his back to the enemy lest they get the upper hand and take him to the ground.

She hadn't seen a weapon in his hand. But she had heard rumors about his kind, had heard they could easily tear a man in half with their bare hands. As much as she would love to see that, she had too many in front of her to hold her focus.

"They're inside the wall!" she screamed as she went into action, swinging her sword, blocking, parrying, slashing.

She racked up one wound for every three she inflicted. The pain was there, but she had to ignore it, had to remember what she was fighting for. A cut, a slash, even broken bones wouldn't stop her from protecting those who had taken her in, cared for her, and treated her as one of their own after her Clan had been taken.

And they had been taken by these assholes, these Elves who thought the world should belong to them, that women were nothing more than property.

Shicks. *Tings*. Grunts. Curses. So many sounds filled the air. Fear burned a path through Valdis's veins while adrenaline filled them with ice.

She wanted to trace her link to Jhelan to see if he was safe, but couldn't take the time without risking becoming too distracted.

A roar came from behind her followed by a pain filled scream that turned to a sickening, gurgling sound.

"Valdis?" Brizio called.

"I'm fine," she called back as she ducked another blow.

A sword slid across her chest but the leather battle vest she'd been fitted with kept the blade from piercing her flesh.

She swung her own sword and made contact with the side of the man's throat, opening his carotid artery. He slapped a hand over the gash, stumbling away, but eventually fell as his life bled out.

Another gust of wind succeeded in knocking the others off their feet. Yet Brizio and Valdis remained standing.

He gripped the front of her vest and attempted to shove her toward the front of the property. "There are too many back here for the two of us," he said.

He no more got the words out of his mouth before someone succeeded in hamstringing him.

With an angry growl, he turned, grabbed his assailant by the shoulder and head, and twisted until the man was looking in the wrong direction before dropping to the ground.

To be that strong... Valdis was lucky enough to be able to yield a sword. If she had any other gifts to aid her, she could help neutralize the numbers.

But as it was, they would have to retreat to join the other guard members fighting in clusters. Because the two of them were no match for the growing numbers that continued to flood from under the wall.

Pandemonium was the only word Valdis could conjure for the scene she found on the front lawn of the Palace. There were so many guards fighting two, three, or four opponents at once. The witches were busy holding the doors closed and fighting elemental magic being blasted from somewhere on the other side.

If the Fae infiltrated, all would be lost.

"We are not trespassers," the woman finally said. "I have received word that one of my descendants could be in trouble."

Jhelan frowned. The only Fairy he was aware of in the territory was his own mate. And if this woman thought he would allow her to harm Valdis in any way, he would prove her wrong with a slice of his blade.

"We are not the enemy. We were sent by the Seelie Court to ensure none of our own were harmed by one of your kind."

"I would never hurt Valdis. She is safe and has been kept so by my people for over a month. She and I have become Bonded."

He held up his arm to reveal the brands he carried that matched Valdis's.

Her eyes dipped to his arm then raised to his face, the same smirk, the same expression on her face.

"The attack has begun," she said as though discussing the weather. "Your kind are attacking the Palace and are a danger to my descendant."

"They are, indeed, Elves, but they are not of our ilk. They are the enemy from a region bent on destruction. They have recruited others to do their bidding. Yes, your descendant is there, but so are families, children, innocents who have done nothing to earn the violence that has been brought to their lives."

The regal woman momentarily closed her eyes. When she opened them, she nodded. "We shall join you. But we will only protect my descendant. A fight among Elves is none of our concern."

He didn't bother mentioning there would be far more beings than simply Elves fighting. If he could get past the Fairy faster and get to his mate, he didn't care about much else. He and his guard would defend the rest of Ahdlai. The Fairies could help watch over Valdis. It was another line of defense for the woman who held his heart and soul in her dainty hands.

"Mount up!" Jhelan called, turning his back on the woman and running for his horse. "The women will ride back with us."

"They're Fae. They'll stab us in the back the moment we turn," Ahdeben nearly spat.

"We will not attack. You are of no concern to us."

Jhelan didn't bother asking the woman's name. It didn't matter. The Fae and Elves had never and *would* never get along. They were born enemies, only neither attacked the other. The Fae simply felt more superior and had staked claim on their own little piece of the planet and allowed no one within their territory. No visitors. No outsiders. No species other than Fae.

Yet they had no trouble traipsing into Elven territory, demanding to be brought to someone who shared the same genes.

There were no full-blooded creatures left on the planet other than humans. All paranormal and supernatural creatures were halflings. There was literally no reason the Fae should believe themselves above all others.

Jhelan climbed into his saddle, then held a hand out, hoisting the woman with one hard pull when she clasped her hand around his forearm. The other men might not like it, but they each followed his orders and allowed the three remaining Fairies to climb onto the back of their horses, tensing when the women wrapped their arms around their waists.

If his load fell off, he wouldn't go back for her. He would continue forward. He would continue to race to get to his mate.

Now that he was no longer facing down his own threat, he focused on his Bond and walked through the battle with her. She had injuries. He could feel the aches, the pain of several cuts along her body feeding through the link.

Her fear was bitter in his mouth, but her strongest emotion was anger. Rage. She wanted revenge. She wanted revenge for what they had done to her, what they had done to her Clan, and what they would continue to do to so many others if they weren't stopped.

It would never stop. The *Ihllr* would never be fully decimated. The best any of them could ask for was to keep their numbers manageable and perhaps someday come to some form of an alliance. They were all of the same species, after all. One would think the Elves would prefer to band together against the threats that loomed over them all like the Strigoi, the Banshees, and so many other soul stealing creatures.

Muscles bunched and released on the horse below him as he pushed his animal harder and faster than he ever had, forcing the animal to race home. A series of hooves slammed into the hardened ground as those who had joined him on his mission chased behind him, keeping pace, pushing their animals as hard.

The woman behind him kept a tight grip around his waist, her chest and torso flat to his back, leaning when he leaned, but she stayed silent.

Even in her silence, he could feel her power begin to flow from her, build, ebb and flow around them as she prepared to use her gifts to push through the crowd in order to get to Valdis.

Jhelan sure as hell hoped none of the Fae women believed they would take Valdis with them when they left. While he would never keep his mate with him against her will, he also would never allow anyone to tear her away from him without a fight if she chose to stay in Ahdlai and in his arms.

Closer. They were getting closer. He could hear the sounds of chaos ahead of them but could not yet see the town. But Jhelan could see the top of the Palace. Not much longer.

Hold on, khaere. *I'm coming.*

He had no idea whether she would hear his words through their Bond or simply detect his presence as he grew near. A sense of relief didn't wash over him from her side. Was she blocking him to focus on the fight? Or was she...

No. He wouldn't entertain the idea. She would survive. Brizio swore to stay by her side, to protect her with his life. Jhelan didn't know the ogre, but felt his words were genuine and had to trust he would keep his word. Hoped and prayed he would keep his word.

The closer they got to town, the louder the sounds of battle grew. Magic was thick in the air and caused the hair to stand on end across his body.

"Unseelie," the woman behind him growled.

Why the hell would the Fae work with Elves? They despised them. And the Unseelie weren't the type to be bought or bribed. If they wanted something, they took it, whether with coercion or magic.

There was another wave of magic in the air, something he'd yet to feel. The witches? Had the others arrived during Jhelan's absence? Or were the four the only ones who were currently struggling to combat the onslaught of the elemental Fae.

A wave of pain hit Jhelan. He doubled, wrapping an arm around his phantom wound.

Valdis.

A blade had made its way through the leather and cut deep through her middle. No. The Universe would not finally send him the most perfect woman for him then take her away in such a short period of time.

With another hard kick, he pushed his horse forward.

The moment they cleared the rows and rows of houses, Jhelan leapt from the back of his beast without waiting for it to stop.

He pulled his sword, his eyes narrowing on Valdis with crystalline focus, and the world felt like it had slowed.

Swinging, stabbing, lobbing heads from bodies. He didn't stop his momentum as he rushed forward, rushed toward Valdis.

But she didn't favor her wound long. Brizio did as he had promised and stayed near, hovering over her as she pushed through the pain and stood again, sword ready, lips peeled back to reveal blood-stained teeth.

His warrior. His incredibly fragile tiny warrior. She would not go down without a fight. He knew that about her. Had known it from the moment they'd met.

Watching her now as she punished the Elf who had struck the blow, he smiled as he continued to cut a path to her.

There were so many of the enemy within the walls. The gates had been blasted outward, like something had pulled it from its hinges yet there were no tools or carts or any form of mechanics visible that could have achieved such a feat.

They didn't have a chance in hell. With the power exerted to blast the doors outward, what else could the Unseelie do?

He finally made it to Valdis's side after what felt like an eternity. Time no longer slowed. It stood still as her eyes locked on his. The silver glow filled her pupils, almost too bright to maintain eye contact.

His warrior mate looked feral. Had there not been a bloody slash across her middle, he might have found her sexy.

The sword gripped in both hands was coated with the blood of their enemy. Her face and any exposed skin were dappled and splattered with droplets and streaks of blood.

Her eyes widened. She lifted her sword. He knew without a word someone was behind him.

Jhelan turned, swinging his sword in an arc…and halted before making contact with the woman from the woods.

"This is my descendant," she declared. "Valdis. I am your great aunt Fallon. We are here to ensure these *people* do not injure you."

There was so much venom in her voice and her gaze when her eyes scanned Jhelan from head to toe, lingering only a moment on his brands before turning back to Valdis.

"There are too many," Valdis said through her labored breathing.

Fallon *tsked* and raised a hand. Those near enough to rush the threesome were lifted from their feet and thrown several yards by a blast of wind that didn't so much as ruffle Valdis's blonde, braided hair.

"Just make sure you don't hurt the wrong people," Valdis said, ready to jump back into battle.

"They are all the wrong people for someone like us," Fallon said.

Valdis looked over her shoulder at her long lost relative. "I lived my whole life without you or the others. We'll be fine without you. If you can't avoid hurting my family, you're free to leave."

Fallon sighed theatrically. But she turned and watched to identify who she was and wasn't supposed to attack.

"The Unseelie. Why in the pits of hades are they here?" Oh, that little piece of news angered Fallon. She turned her ire on the Fae intent on ensuring the *Vhtir* were wiped from the planet.

Throwing her arms out to her sides, Fallon moved toward the Unseelie.

Brizio and his witch companions had been joined by more members of their Coven. Guard members were battling *Ihllr* Elves and Shape-Shifters Jhelan didn't recognize, presumably from another Pack.

They had to end this before the sun set. Because Jhelan wouldn't put it past the enemy to have recruited vampires, as well.

Brizio and Jhelan stayed as close to Valdis as possible, but she didn't bother checking for back up as she charged after anyone who wasn't *Vhtir* or ally.

Her head whipped around as she followed the path of six *Ihllr* assholes.

"They're in the Palace!"

Without waiting for anyone else, she charged forward, ready to protect the King, Queen, and any residents holed up inside.

Jhelan slashed his sword across the throat of his current opponent and chased after her. But his path was cut off by an Unseelie whose eyes blazed as bright as the sun. She grinned then crouched, touching her fingertips to the ground.

The earth began to shake beneath Jhelan's feet until it was a struggle to remain standing.

He had to get past this Fairy. Had to get inside the Palace. Had to get to his mate's side. Because he hadn't seen any other of their people running with her.

She was now inside with six enemy combatants. She would go toe to toe with six men who towered over her by no less than half a foot, six men intent on slaughtering anyone who stood in the way of their goal of taking over Ahdlai.

She was on her own.

Chapter Seventeen

Valdis ached. The cuts and gashes covering her body stung and throbbed. Her muscles screamed in protest.

But she wouldn't stop. She had trained for this very moment.

She watched in shock as six men rushed up the front steps and inside the Palace. The King and Queen were in there with the residents. She knew without a doubt the King would swing his sword to defend his mate and his people.

But he would be outnumbered.

Even with her at his back, they would both still be outnumbered, but it was better than sitting by while these evil bastards killed more innocent people.

As she'd fought outside, she couldn't help but wonder if she was going crazy. More and more *Ihllr* Elves continued to appear from under the wall. When the door had been blown open by magic, even more had poured onto the lawn.

How many were there in Mhahzin? Or had they developed a village nearby and built their numbers alongside those living in the southern region?

Mhahzin was paradise. The people there were peaceful. They were farmers and had been the largest contributors to those in the north when humans had destroyed the planet.

Until the Elves fractured into different groups.

As it was in every species, every population of humans and otherwise, there would always be those who were power hungry, greedy, who would do anything to be on top.

It was no different now than it was then.

With a screech, she lunged at the closest man and swung her sword. He turned at her war cry and raised his own sword, blocking the blade before it could make contact.

She was locked in battle, the sounds of metal hitting metal a background to the shocked cries as the five others found those hiding in the basement.

"They're inside the Palace!" she screamed again as she had outside.

As Valdis ducked and thrust her blade, the ground below her began to shake. It was low at first, like the rumble of thunder.

The tip of her sword pierced the man's chest, bursting through his leather battle armor and lodging deep inside his body.

She yanked it free with a grunt and kicked him, knocking him down and out of her way. But when she tried to get to the residents and the Royal family, those mild tremors grew until she had to hold onto the walls and any furniture within reach to remain on her feet.

Magic. The Unseelie Fae were using elemental magic to help the *Ihllr*. She had no idea what they thought they would get out of it, but had no time to dwell. She had to get the innocent people of Ahdlai before it was too late.

Hand on the wall, she rounded the corner and nearly fell down the stairs as the ground continued to shake and walls around her rattled. Each hit against the steps sent more pain radiating through her body. She would have broken bones and require stitches when this was over. But for now, the adrenaline was keeping her going, forcing her body to continue moving, forcing her brain to block out what she knew later would be agony.

Fighting had ensued below. Turning the corner, she gave her eyes time to take in the situation to avoid slashing at the wrong person.

The King and Queen both wielded weapons and were the only thing keeping the enemy from the residents huddled in a corner. Some whimpered, children cried, but most watched with wide, shock filled eyes.

The quakes had started slowly but cut off so suddenly Valdis was pitched forward. She used the momentum to attack her next foe.

Without her battle cry, he wasn't aware the cavalry in the shape of a small woman had arrived at his back.

She swung hard, decapitating him with one swing. Her gag reflex kicked in at the hot spray of blood that splashed across her face, but she didn't have time to entertain it. She would puke later. For now, there were four more who needed the same form of punishment.

The King had taken out another.

Three more.

The Queen wasn't faring so well. Her beautiful gown was covered with blood, rips and tears indicated a good portion of it was her own.

Leaving the King to deal with his two, Valdis rushed forward to protect the Queen, even if it meant giving her own life.

As a sword swung toward Queen Ahlmeda's throat, Valdis threw her own sword forward and deflected it, immediately parrying and kicking at him to put more distance between the fight and the Queen.

Another man fell. Two left. And two fighters. They had a chance. A damn good one. Because the King flourished his weapon as though he had been a guard at one time.

One left.

And he was all Valdis's.

This asshole wasn't so easy to take down. He was fast. And scored more hits on Valdis than she was able to block.

"Enough!" someone screamed from the back.

It was more than enough. But the enemy would never stop. They had to be stopped. And Valdis sure as hell hoped she would be the victor. Jhelan would never forgive himself if she were to go down and he hadn't been by her side.

And Brizio. Since he hadn't followed her inside, she could only assume he was either fighting a large number or he, himself, had been slain.

So many dead. So much blood soaked into the beautiful lawn surrounding the Palace.

They had lived in peace. These people had merely wanted to live their lives and be happy. And that life had been turned on its head by one ruthless leader.

Valdis's swings began to slow as fatigue gnawed at her, as her muscles begged for a break. But there were no breaks to be had, not when a sword longer than her arm was being swung at her head.

Her foe stiffened suddenly, his eyes going wide. Then the tip of a sword appeared through his chest, sliding further before being ripped out. It took the Elf a moment to realize he'd been stabbed as he stared down at the growing crimson stain on his chest.

And then he dropped to his knees.

Jhelan stood behind him, his breath coming fast, blood coating every part of him that she could see.

Thank Mother Universe. He was alive. He looked as badly injured as she felt, but he was alive and on his own two feet.

"How many more outside?" she asked, sucking in breath after breath as her heart threatened to burst through her ribcage.

"The Seelie have it under control."

"Why are they here?" Valdis asked.

"For you. I think they will try to talk you into returning with them."

She grunted and shook her head.

She wouldn't leave Ahdlai. She wouldn't leave Jhelan. This was her home now. Jhelan was her home.

He checked her over, but she waved him away. "Queen Ahlmeda is injured. Check her and find the healer."

"I'm here," the healer said.

She stood from the back of the crowd and made her way forward. Of course she would be hidden away. They needed her alive to tend to those who had endured grave injuries during the battle.

Looking over the Queen, she shot glances in Valdis's direction, scanning her from head to toe quickly before refocusing on the Ahdlai's ruler.

Valdis took a moment to check on the residents. None looked as though they had been harmed. A small face appeared around the shoulder of one of the women, a sweet face that made everything she had just gone through worth every second. Flora. She was alive. She was safe. She hadn't been harmed or taken by the evil bastards who would...

She refused to think about it.

Flora smiled at Valdis through tears, then pushed through the crowd until she could reach for Valdis.

"I'm all yucky, honey. I promise to give you the biggest hug in the whole world after I've showered and changed."

Bending forward, she pressed a kiss to Flora's forehead and nodded for her to return to the rest of the group for now.

Jhelan gripped Valdis by the shoulders and turned her toward him roughly. His hand roamed her face, her head, her neck, then down both arms.

"I'm fine," she said.

"You're far from fine."

"You don't look too much better, *khaere*."

Jhelan's hands stilled and he stared down into Valdis's eyes.

"You called me..." His words trailed off and he crashed his mouth onto hers, gently wrapping his arms around her back to drag her closer to him.

She knew it hurt him because the move hurt like hell to her. But it was worth it. They had both made it alive. They had made it back to each other.

I will always return to you.

He'd told her that. She'd believed him then, and she knew after today, she would believe those words for the rest of her life.

When he pulled back, they both nearly stumbled. They had been leaning on each other, using the other to remain upright.

"How many have we lost?" King Nhaeem asked.

"I have not received a number. I joined Valdis to come to your side as soon as I could."

"Thank you," the King said.

Shock rippled through her brands when the King of the northern region of Ahdlai bowed his head at the head of his Royal guard.

"You and your mate saved our lives. You saved all our lives."

"My mate did that. I merely killed the last standing," Jhelan said.

"We need to check on everyone else. Are Ihsander and Ahdeben okay? Brizio? The witches?"

Jhelan shook his head. "I didn't take the time to check."

He wrapped an arm around her shoulders as she wrapped hers around his waist. They used each other to stay on their feet and climbed the stairs to the main floor of the Palace.

The body of the first *Ihllr* Elf she'd slain lay on the marble floor, blood forming a crimson pool around him.

They stepped over him and continued outside in time to see those who had survived from the enemy camp fleeing through the destroyed gate.

"Should we chase after them? They could recover and attack again," Valdis said.

"No. We all need rest. We need to bury our dead and grieve. Then we'll return to our duties of keeping our town safe. And I think it's time to talk to the King and Queen about increasing the wall to include the houses of the residents."

That had been her idea. But so much had happened since that day they hadn't had a moment to explore it any further.

The lawn was...

She had no words.

So much blood had been spilled. So many dead from both sides. The coppery scent filled the air and felt like it coated her lungs.

The Unseelie were long gone, but the Seelie Fae, those who had come searching for her, lingered nearby, looks of pure disdain on each of their faces.

"Mother Universe," she muttered as she and Jhelan slowly descended the steps.

She'd seen death. She'd seen violence. But she had never witnessed the level of destruction and violence of today's fight. The evidence of battle was everywhere she looked.

"Do you see them? Do you see Ihsander? Ahdeben? Brizio?"

He shook his head as they moved around bodies, checked on those that were alive or looked as though they were breathing. They rolled the dead onto their backs to check each and every face for Jhelan's closest friends, including Prince Ahrkyn.

Valdis had been intent on protecting the King and Queen and the innocent residents but hadn't given a second thought to the Prince. He might have been one of the casualties.

"Jhelan!" a voice called.

Ihsander jogged from around a tree. He looked as bad as everyone else still standing.

"Thank the Mother you're alive."

He shocked the hell out of Valdis when he hugged her before turning to Jhelan to drag him into a masculine, back slapping hug.

"Ahdeben? Ahrkyn?" Jhelan asked.

"Wounded but okay. They're helping Brizio look for survivors of either side."

Valdis had never experienced the degree of wariness she felt now. But the day was far from over. They would have to bury the dead, make an account of anyone missing, tend to numerous wounds, and attempt to fortify the destroyed gate.

And she wanted nothing more than to crawl in bed with Jhelan wrapped around her to sleep for the next week. Or more.

It was well past dark by the time they'd tallied and buried the dead. The *Ihllr* had suffered far more casualties than the *Vhtir*. But that didn't make him feel any better.

Why the hell were they always fighting each other? There were enough struggles and enough enemies in the world that the Elves should have been banding together.

All it took was one person with delusions of grandeur to destroy any sense of unity or peace.

The destroyed gates had been repaired by the witches and Seelie Fae combining their magic. It would still need to be replaced, but it would hold for the night.

The witches had also cast a barrier spell around the entirety of the Palace and the town of Ahdlai. As much as he would prefer the entire region to be safeguarded, there were those who chose to live outside of society who could be affected undeservedly.

"Your mate looks like she's about to fall over," Ihsander announced.

Jhelan turned to watch as Valdis staggered as she helped yet another injured guard to see the healer. She hadn't had her own wounds tended yet was ensuring everyone else was cared for.

It was another reason Jhelan thanked the Mother for sending her to him.

"She won't stop," Jhelan said. "I have tried to get her to rest several times. Something is driving her."

"It will drive her to an early grave if she isn't careful. She needs to have some of those wounds checked," Ahdeben said.

Jhelan gave a grunt and followed his mate into the Palace and downstairs to the healer's surgery. There were so many men down there, *his* men, the men he had trained, young Elves who were not full members of the guard yet had been forced to battle for their first time.

He tried to see what she saw, tried to understand why she continued to help others seek help when she was injured herself.

Jhelan had several deep cuts, but his accelerated healing had already staunched the flow of blood. Hers would do the same. The ones he could see through rips in her clothing and battle vest continued to ooze blood, though not at a rate to alarm him.

These men, those she had put before her own needs, were critical. She was triaging needs, bringing those who could die or lose a limb without immediate care, those who suffered far too many deep wounds for their healing abilities to tend to them all.

Her wounds were not life threatening. Painful, he was sure. But she wanted to save as many as possible...because she was unable to save her last Clan.

Brizio's heavy steps thumped on the wooden stairs as he carried a male over his shoulder.

"This is the last survivor we found. His wounds don't look serious, but he is not waking."

He set him on the floor as there was no more space on gurneys or counters.

Jhelan wrapped a hand around Valdis's arm and pulled her away. "There's nothing left for us to do. Let's go home, clean the blood, and I'll see if there are any wounds that can't wait until morning."

He didn't trust his own skills to stitch her if required. But he had enough bandaging and other supplies if she could get through the night without care from the town's only healer.

With nothing more to do, she looked up at him and gave a slow blink as she swayed on her feet. She would fall asleep the moment her head hit the pillow.

They trudged up the stairs through the house, across the blood-stained lawn.

Fallon and the other members of her Court waited near the gate. "It's time to join your own kind, Valdis."

There were times when Jhelan wished he could guard Valdis from any and every discomfort. Then there were times like now when he was just as happy to simply stand by and watch as his mate squared her shoulders and looked directly into the eyes of a woman she had never met and hadn't bothered seeking her out until today.

"I have been on my own since my parents were killed, yet you didn't bother looking for me. I lived in the woods with the humans, yet you never extended an invitation to live with my own kind," she said, mimicking Fallon. "This is my family. We might share the same blood line, but we are not the same. It was nice to meet you, and I thank you for your help against the Unseelie, but I'm not going anywhere except to the home I share with my mate where we'll shower and drop into bed."

Fallon's chin lifted and she looked down her nose at Valdis. "You would prefer to live among thieves and beggars than your own kind?"

Jhelan felt a rush of anger through the Bond he shared with Valdis a second before she took a step closer to Fallon.

"Let me say it again. We might be of the same blood line, but we're not family. We're nothing alike. Thank you again for helping. But if you plan on insulting the people who have done more for me in the past two months than you have in my lifetime, you're free to head right back to your almighty Court."

There was a brief moment where Jhelan feared Fallon and the other members of the Court she'd brought with her would use magic to force Valdis to join her. But when sadness entered her eyes and she sighed, he nearly sagged with relief. He didn't think he had enough energy or strength left in his body to fight anyone else.

"The invitation remains open. Should you ever wish to rejoin your family Court, you will simply only need to send word of your intentions and I will send someone to retrieve you."

Fallon turned and began to head toward the woods. Before she and the others disappeared into the darkness, she turned and looked at Valdis over her shoulder. "I didn't know."

"What?" Valdis said.

"I only learned of your existence recently. I would have searched for you sooner."

With that, she practically floated away on the breeze, not a sound made as she entered the woods and blended into the darkness.

"I want to go home," Valdis said.

"Me, too." He took her hand to lead her to the house they shared and fight the urge to carry her the way he had so many times in the beginning.

As tired as she was, she probably wouldn't fight him, but he wasn't sure he had the strength to lift his arms, let alone lift her.

The house was dark as they stepped through the front door. He was mildly surprised none of the trespassers had bothered to trash any of the homes or raid them for food or other commodities.

Without turning on any lights, he continued through the house, his hand wrapped tightly around hers, until they stepped into the bathroom. He flipped the switch to illuminate that room. He needed to be able to see every inch of Valdis clearly.

She hissed in a breath and tensed as he began to remove first the leather vest then pulled the tunic over her head. Jhelan growled low in his throat at how many cuts she'd endured, but none looked life-threatening.

Her pants went next. A few knicks and a lot of bruising, but nothing that required stitches. She had fared far better today than she had during her last run in with the *Ihllr*.

"Your turn," she said.

Lifting onto her toes, she tried to help remove his vest and shirt, but he could see the pain etched in every line of her face as she stretched her arms over her head. He had grown accustomed to pain, had grown accustomed to the many injuries he would endure when the guard came across the enemy in the forest.

This, all of this, was new to her.

Then again, she had fought to protect her previous Clan. She must have suffered plenty of times before today. His little warrior clenched her teeth and pushed through the pain as she continued to help him remove his clothing as he had for her.

When they were both naked and had checked to make sure neither would need to visit the healer immediately, Jhelan turned the knobs to fill the tub with water. No way could either of them submerge themselves without causing further pain, but they needed to remove as much blood and debris as possible before dressing the wounds.

He grabbed several cloths from the closet and as each turned first pink then deep red, he would rinse them in the tub to start all over again until they could no longer find any clear spots on the cotton.

They took turns cleaning each other, gingerly running the cloth across each other's flesh, yet Jhelan couldn't summon an ounce of lust. His beautiful mate was standing before him naked, but her body was covered and crisscrossed with so many wounds he wondered if she wouldn't be covered in scars.

It didn't matter. He didn't care how she looked. He loved her. He loved her so much it hurt. So much his heart felt at times as though it would burst through his chest with fullness.

"I don't think I've ever been so tired in my life. I thought training was hard." She shook her head.

"You got breaks while training," Jhelan reminded her. "You've been going nonstop for hours. I'm exhausted, too. Everyone is."

Once his mate was cleaned and the worst of her injuries bandaged, he cupped her face in his hands. "You were amazing. But you scared the shit out of me."

She gripped his wrists, keeping his hands on her.

"I was so scared I wouldn't see you again. I thought…I was afraid I would walk outside to find you dead on the ground somewhere. But I felt you. I felt you through the brands. And it kept me strong, helped me keep going when I was ready to fall over or give up trying to make a difference," Valdis said.

"You saved the Queen. You understand the gravity of that, don't you?"

She shrugged. "I was saving an innocent person. She just happened to be the Queen of Ahdlai."

He huffed a laugh. "You never cease to amaze me. Every time I think I know you, you say or do something that shocks me. Not many people are capable of that."

Her shoulders rose and fell again, and she dropped her arms to her sides. "I'm strange. I'm aware."

Jhelan chuckled and turned Valdis toward the door, then nearly pushed her toward the bed. She didn't need much persuasion.

Neither of them donned any clothing before dropping heavily onto the bed. The bathroom light was still on, yet Jhelan didn't have the energy to stand, walk the few feet there, and turn it off.

Besides, he wouldn't see anything with his eyes closed.

"So help me, Mother Universe, if a single person knocks on this door or tries to cause any more trouble before noon tomorrow, I might go full berserker."

He laughed softly and gently laid a hand on her hip to tug her closer to him so he could spoon behind her. They might not have been able to make love tonight, but he needed her as close as possible.

Her butt was cradled by his groin, the backs of her thighs lined along the fronts of his, her back against his chest. He wanted to hug her to him tighter but worried about hurting her. Or himself. He would feel every single wound he'd racked up tomorrow.

But for tonight, he would rest with his mate in his arms. He would rest knowing they had done everything in their power to keep their people safe.

He would rest knowing his mate had saved the Queen and the people of Ahdlai.

Chapter Eighteen

"Kneel," the King ordered.

Nerves sent Valdis's stomach into a flurry of butterflies. She had been called before the King and Queen. The Royal guard stood at her back, dressed head to toe in their battle gear, their swords strapped to their backs.

Had she done something wrong? Had she killed an innocent bystander or a guard member she hadn't met?

"Because of your actions, my beautiful mate will remain at my side for centuries to come. The residents of Ahdlai survived an attack unlike any we have endured. You nearly sacrificed yourself for those whom now call you friend, sister...daughter. They now call you family. You were given a choice by the Seelie, your own people, your own bloodline, yet you chose to remain with us. For all those reasons, I have an important request to ask of you."

On her knee, Valdis frowned up at the King in confusion.

"Ask, Your Highness."

"My wife has demanded I name you her personal guard. We have not had a female member of the Royal guard since the death of Jhelan's mother. And we have not met any who rose to the high standards of the position since that day. But your bravery and willingness to put all others above yourself far exceeds your small stature. So, my request is would you please be willing to honor my wife by being her personal Royal guard? You will stay by her side when she leaves the safety of the wall, you will be at her side should we endure another attack."

"You want me to join the Royal guard."

She repeated his words because she was having a difficult time making her brain comprehend what he was asking her.

"Yes," the Queen said.

"Should your answer be no, you will still be welcome to remain in Ahdlai and at Jhelan's side. You will still be welcome to patrol with the Royal guard, although I believe your mate will demand you patrol with him. But should your answer be yes, you may ask any favor of me that is in your heart."

"I would like a wall built around the town," she blurted before answering. "I would like the residents who live here to receive the same barrier of protection as yourself and your family. Should you agree to this condition, then I whole heartedly agree to perform the duties of personal guard to your wife, Her Highness Queen Ahlmeda."

The Queen grinned with joy. The King's smile was slow but appeared as he nodded. "It will be done. We will begin building an outer wall to encase all residents who live within the town of Ahdlai proper immediately."

A single Elven word – unknown to her – roared behind her from the collection of the guard. She looked over her shoulder to see them slam fists to their chests in unison. They had accepted her as one of their own. She had a family. She had a mate. And now she had a role in this place she called home.

Her eyes scanned the crowd until she found Jhelan standing in the back, the most tender and proud smile on his face.

She knew he feared for her new role, could feel his emotions throbbing through her brands, but could also feel the joy and love through those brands.

Turning back to the Royal couple, she began to feel awkward. "Uh, may I stand?"

"Of course," King Nhaeem said.

"We mourned our dead for a week. But tonight…we celebrate. We will celebrate the lives of those lost, celebrate for those left behind, celebrate the future of Ahdlai, and celebrate your future with us," the Queen declared.

The crowd behind her erupted in cheer, then hands were on her, dragging her through the throng of men, clapping her on the back as if she were one of them, shaking her hand, welcoming her to the fold, congratulating her.

Until she was delivered into Jhelan's waiting arms. He kissed her deeply, sensually, a kiss that curled her toes and heated her blood.

When the night was over, the two of them would celebrate in their own way.

"What exactly does a celebration here entail?" she asked when Jhelan finally pulled away.

"Feasting. Drinking until you can't stand. And a lot of hazing by the rest of your new brothers-at-arms."

"I'm scared to ask about the hazing," she said before rising onto her toes and pressing a quick kiss to his lips.

Valdis rolled over and groaned. Jhelan hadn't lied when he'd said they would drink until they couldn't stand. She'd drank wine in her lifetime, but had never drank so much that the world felt as though it spun so fast she needed to hold on something sturdy to avoid flying off.

Her head throbbed, her stomach rolled, and there was a taste that reminded her of the smell of decaying meat in her mouth.

"Good morning," Jhelan said from beside her.

With another groan, she lifted an arm and threw it over her eyes to block out the offensive sun pouring through the open curtains.

"You'll feel better after you get some food in your stomach."

She couldn't hold back the gag.

He also hadn't lied about feasting. She had eaten until her stomach was stretched to its limits. But they had truly celebrated. They had toasted the fallen brothers, toasted those like Brizio and his Coven who had come to their aid, and toasted each other.

And they had toasted her.

That had felt awkward. She was not the only one who'd fought so fiercely. She'd gone to the Queen's aid but knew any single one of the guards would have done the same had they gotten inside before her. It was only fate that she'd been able to rush past the Unseelie.

Or…perhaps her gift was immunity to their powers. She might have been shaken by the quake caused by their magic, but none of them had been able to stop any of her movements with anything they had thrown her way. It wasn't nearly as impressive as the things the rest of the Fae or witches or even the Elves could do, but it was something.

As she laid there, doing her best to keep her stomach from rejecting anything that might have been left inside of her, she rolled that last thought over and over in her head.

She hadn't been stopped by magic. She had no offensive gifts, but if she was right and her gift was some form of shield, it was fated that she was the one to make it to the Queen first.

Mother Universe had given her the gift that would be needed most as she knew the outcome of all things to come.

"I have a gift," she muttered to herself.

"What?"

She removed her arm and rolled her head to look at her mate. "The only thing that affected me when the Unseelie attacked was the movement of the ground. Had the magic stopped me, I wouldn't have made it to the Queen. She and the others would have been killed. My gift is a shield against dark magic."

His smile was soft as he rested his palm against her cheek.

"I have thanked the Mother countless times since the moment I realized how deeply my feelings for you went. And now I have another thing to thank her for. She gifted you with the tool needed to protect our people. You were the only one who could. You were the only one able to get past the Unseelie. You trained hard and were able to best your opponents." He leaned forward and pressed his lips to her forehead. "You would have impressed my parents more than any other being on this planet."

Such a sweet statement, yet it sent pride to her heart. After all he had told her about his amazing mother and his brave father, she felt she truly deserved a place in Jhelan's heart and in his life.

"When I accepted the role as personal guard to the Queen, you all slammed a fist to your chest and shouted a word. What did you say? What was the word?"

His smile grew. He pushed hair behind her ear as his gaze held hers.

"Family. We shouted family."

Family. She had a family. She had lost her Clan, but she had never truly felt like she had belonged there with them. She cared for them, of course, had protected them to the best of her abilities. But she had never felt the deep connection she felt here with these people and with Jhelan.

She had found her family. She had found her home.

She had found where her heart and soul belonged.

Thank you for reading *Soul Alliance*. I hope you loved Jhelan and Valdis as much as I do!

If you liked this book, please consider rating or reviewing it on Amazon and/or Goodreads. Your support will help other readers find the panthers, bears, wolves, and more of Cedar Hill!

Thank you!

About the Author

Lynn Howard lives in Cedar Hill, MO, where all her sexy Shifters exist. She lives and breathes hot Alpha males and sassy, brassy females. She feels the most at home knee deep in mud and chicken muck and prefers to be outside under the stars, cuddled up under a blanket in front of a bonfire.

When not typing away or feeding her chickens, you can find her fantasizing about hot country boys for her next book or wandering the woods in search of wildlife. She loves all animals and insects…except spiders. Her favorite foot accessory is barefoot and she owns at least thirty sets of salt-n-pepper shakers, yet only uses one.

Gray's Wolf is the first in the Big River Pack series. And just like in Gray's Wolf, there are more hot country boy Shifters just waiting to their turn for a little love and romance.

Reading Order

Big River pack:
Gray's Wolf
Micah's Match
Emory's Mate
Reed's Girl
Tristan's Voice

Blackwater Clan:
Colton's Kitty

Noah's Fire
Carter's Devotion
Luke's Redemption

Ravenwood Pride:
Braxton's Warrior
Aron's Element
Daxon's Heart
Mason's Princess

Morse Pack:
Koda's Challenge
Auddi's Destiny
Zeke's Revelation

Shifter Council Executioners:
Shift in Priority
Shift in Focus

Other Titles by Lynn Howard:
Soul Surrendered
Laken (Immortally Yours)
Zac (Immortally Yours)
Her Heart to Mend (A Contemporary Romance)

www.ingramcontent.com/pod-product-compliance
Lightning Source LLC
Chambersburg PA
CBHW061237170626
46809CB00007B/2720